Now he didn't know what to think.

All he knew was that nothing had changed for him since last Friday night. One look from those incredible eyes of hers and he'd been right back there on that dance floor, his body consumed by the need to sweep her off into bed.

Bed? He almost laughed at that notion. A bed would not do. This all-consuming passion he was suffering from demanded a much faster, harder surface to pin her to. A wall. A floor. This desk, even…

9 to 5

**Getting to know him in the boardroom...
and the bedroom!**

**A secret romance, a forbidden affair,
a thrilling attraction...**

What happens when two people work together and
simply can't help falling in love—
no matter how hard they try to resist?

Find out in our new series of stories
set against working backgrounds.

This month, top author Miranda Lee rips the lid off
one hot after-hours affair!

BEDDED
BY THE BOSS

BY
MIRANDA LEE

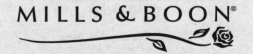

MILLS & BOON®

First published in Great Britain 2004
Harlequin Mills & Boon Limited,
Eton House, 18-24 Paradise Road, Richmond, Surrey TW9 1SR

© Miranda Lee 2004

ISBN 0 263 83792 0

Set in Times Roman 10½ on 12¼ pt.
01-1204-41454

Printed and bound in Spain
by Litografia Rosés, S.A., Barcelona

CHAPTER ONE

'SO WHAT would *you* like in your Christmas stocking, Jessie? I'm going present shopping tomorrow. There's only just over two weeks till Christmas and I hate leaving things to the last moment.'

Jessie stopped applying her mascara for a second to smile wryly across the kitchen table at her elderly friend—and landlady.

'Do you know a shop which sells men?' she asked with a mischievous sparkle in her dark brown eyes.

Dora's own eyes widened. '*Men?* You told me just ten minutes ago that you thought most men were sleazebags and you were better off without one in your life.'

Jessie shrugged. 'That was ten minutes ago. Getting myself dolled up like this tonight reminded me of when I was young and carefree and didn't know the truth about the opposite sex. What I wouldn't give to be that girl again, just for one night, going out with some gorgeous guy on a hot date.'

'And if that fantasy came true,' Dora asked, still with a sceptical expression on her face, 'where would this gorgeous guy be taking you?'

'Oh, somewhere really swish for drinks and dinner, then on to a nightclub for some dirty dancing.' *After which he'd whip me back to his bachelor pad and...*

This last thought startled Jessie. In all honesty, ever since she'd had Emily, she hadn't missed men one bit. Hadn't felt like being with one at all.

Now, suddenly, the thought of having some gorgeous guy's arms around her again was quite pleasurable. *More* than pleasurable, actually. Almost a necessity.

Her female hormones, it seemed, had finally been jump-started again.

Her sigh carried a measure of frustration. And irritation. It was something she could do without. Men complicated things. They always did.

Useless creatures, all of them.

Except in that one department!

Now that her hormones were hopping again, she had to admit there was nothing to compare with the pleasure of being with a man who was a good lover.

Emily's father had been pretty good in bed. But he'd also been a feckless, reckless fool whose wildly adventurous spirit had finally been the death of him, snowboarding his stupid way off a mountain and into a crevasse even before Jessie had discovered she was having his baby.

Jessie had finally come to realise at the wise old age of twenty-eight that the members of the opposite sex who were good in bed were rarely good at commitment. Usually, they were charming scoundrels. She suspected that even if Lyall had lived, he would not have stuck by her and his baby.

No, she was better off without men in her life, in any capacity. For now, anyway. Emily was still only four and very impressionable. The last thing she needed was for her mummy to start dating guys who were only interested in one thing. There was no future in that. And no happiness.

Men could indulge in no-strings sex without suffering any lasting emotional damage. Women, not so easily.

Jessie had taken a long time to get over Lyall, both his death and the discovery she'd made afterwards that she hadn't been the only girl in his life.

'What I really want for Christmas more than anything,' she said firmly as she packed her make-up essentials into her black evening bag, 'is a decent job in an advertising agency.'

Jessie had worked as a graphic artist before she'd fallen pregnant, with an eye to eventually being promoted to the position of creative designer. She hadn't wanted to spend the rest of her life bringing other people's ideas to life; or having them take the credit when she improved on their designs. Jessie knew she had considerable creative talent and dreamt of heading her own advertising team one day; being up close and personal when the presentations were made; getting the accolades herself—plus the bonuses—when she secured a prestigious account for Jackson & Phelps.

That was the advertising agency she'd worked for back then. One of Sydney's biggest and best.

Having Emily, however, had rearranged her priorities in life. She *had* planned on going back to Jackson & Phelps after her maternity leave was up. But when the time came, she'd found she didn't want to put her baby daughter into day-care. She wanted to stay home and take care of Emily herself.

She'd thought she could work from home, free-lance. She had her own computer and all the right software. But a downturn in the economy had meant that advertising budgets were cut and lots of graphic artists were out of work. Freelance work became a pipedream.

Jessie had been forced to temporarily receive state benefits, and to move from the trendy little flat she'd been renting. Luckily, she found accommodation with Dora, a very nice lady with a very nice home in Roseville, a leafy northern Sydney suburb on the train line.

Dora had had a granny flat built on the back when her mother—now deceased—had come to live with her. It was only one-bedroomed, but it had its own bathroom and a spacious kitchen-cum-living room which opened out into the large and secure back yard. Just the thing for a single mum with an active toddler. Emily had turned one by then and was already walking.

The rent Dora charged Jessie was also very reasonable, in exchange for which Jessie helped Dora with the heavy housework and the garden.

But money was still tight. There was never much left over each fortnight. Treats were a rarity. Presents were always cheap little things, both on birthdays and at Christmas. Last Christmas hadn't been a big problem. Emily hadn't been old enough at three to understand that all her gifts had come from a bargain-basement store.

But Jessie had realised at the time that by this coming Christmas, Emily would be far more knowing.

As much as Jessie had enjoyed being a full-time mother at home, the necessities of life demanded that she get off welfare and go back to work. So last January, Jessie had enrolled Emily in a nearby day-care centre and started looking for a job.

Unfortunately, not with great success in her chosen field.

Despite her having her name down at several employment agencies and going for countless interviews, no one in advertising, it seemed, wanted to hire a graphic artist who was a single mum and who had been out of the workforce for over three years.

For a while, earlier this year, she'd done a simply awful—though lucrative—job, working for a private investigator. The ad in the paper had said it was for the position of receptionist. No experience required, just good presentation and a nice phone voice. When she'd got there, she was told the receptionist job had been taken, and she was offered investigative work instead.

Basically, she was sent out as a decoy to entrap men who were suspected by their partners of being unfaithful. She'd be given the time and place—always a pub or a bar—plus a short biography and photo of the target. Her job had required her to dress sexily, make contact, then flirt enough for the target to show his true colours. Once she'd gathered sufficient evidence via the sleek, hi-tech mobile phone which the PI supplied—its video recording was excellent—Jessie would use the excuse of going to the powder room, then disappear.

It had only taken Jessie half a dozen such encounters before she quit. Maybe if, just once, one target had resisted her charms and shown himself to be an honourable man, she might have continued. But no! Each time, the sleazebag—and brother, they were all sleazebags!—wasted no time in not only chatting her up but also propositioning her in no uncertain terms. Each time she'd dashed for the ladies', feeling decidedly dirty.

After that low-life experience, she'd happily taken a waitressing job at a local restaurant. Because of Emily, however, Jessie refused to work at night or at the weekends, when the tips might have been better, so her take-home pay wasn't great. On top of that, her expenses had gone up. Even with her government subsidy for being a single parent, having Emily in day-care five days a week was not cheap.

The only bonus was that Emily adored going to her pre-school. Jessie sometimes felt jealous over how much her daughter loved the teachers there, and the other kids. She'd grown up so much during this past year.

Too much.

She was now four, going on fourteen.

Last weekend, she'd begun asking questions about her father. And had not been impressed when her mother tried to skirt around the subject. A flustered Jessie had been pinned down and forced to tell Emily the truth. That her daddy had died in a tragic accident before she was born. And no, her mummy and her daddy had not been married at the time.

'So you and Daddy aren't divorced,' she'd stunned Jessie by saying. 'He's not ever coming back, like Joel's daddy came back.'

Joel was Emily's best friend at pre-school.

'No, Emily,' Jessie had told her daughter in what she'd hoped was the right sombre and sympathetic tone. 'Your daddy is never coming back. He's in heaven.'

'Oh,' Emily had said, and promptly went off, frowning.

Jessie had found her in a corner of the back yard, having a serious conversation with her life-sized baby doll—the one Dora had given her for her fourth birthday in August. Emily had fallen ominously silent when her mother approached. Jessie had been very relieved when her daughter had finally looked up, smiled brightly and asked her if they could go and see Santa at K-Mart that afternoon, because she had to tell him what she wanted for Christmas before it was too late.

Clearly, Emily was too young at four to be devastated by the discovery that the father she had never known was in heaven.

But Emily's reminder that Christmas was coming up fast—along with the fact that Jessie already knew the main present Emily wanted for Christmas—was what had brought Jessie to make the decision to do one more wretched job for Jack Keegan. The PI had said to give him a call if she ever needed some extra cash. Which she surely did, because a Felicity Fairy doll was the most expensive doll to hit the toy market in ages. Jessie would need all of the four-hundred-dollar fee she would earn tonight to buy the darned doll, along with all its accompaniments. There was a fairy palace, a magic horse and a sparkling wardrobe full of clothes.

Speaking of clothes...

Jessie stood up and smoothed down the short skirt of the black crêpe halter-necked dress she'd dragged out of her depleted wardrobe for tonight's job. It was the classiest, sexiest dress she owned, but it was six years old and Jessie feared it was beginning to look it.

'Are you sure this dress is OK?' she asked Dora in a fretful tone. 'It's getting awfully old.'

'It's fine,' Dora reassured. 'And not out of fashion at all. That style is timeless. You look gorgeous, Jessie. Very sexy. Like a model.'

'Who, me? Don't be ridiculous, Dora. I know I've got a good figure, but the rest of me is pretty ordinary. Without my make-up on, no man would give me a second glance. And my hair is an uncontrollable disaster if I don't drag it back or put it up.'

'You underestimate your attractiveness, Jessie.'

In every way, Dora thought to herself.

Jessie's figure wasn't just good, it was spectacular, the kind of body you often saw in underwear advertisements these days. Full breasts. Tiny waist. Slender hips and long legs. They looked even longer in the high, strappy shoes Jessie was wearing tonight.

It was true that her face wasn't traditionally pretty. Her mouth was too wide, her jaw too square and her nose slightly too long. But anchored on either side of that nose were widely set, exotically shaped dark brown eyes which flashed and smouldered with sensual promise, the kind of eyes that drew men like magnets.

As for her hair…Dora would have killed for hair like Jessie's when she'd been younger.

Blue-black, thick and naturally curly, when left down it cascaded around her face and shoulders in glorious disarray. Up, it defied restraint, with bits and pieces escaping, making her look even sexier, if that was possible.

Dora hadn't been surprised when that private detective had snapped Jessie up to do decoy work for him. She was the perfect weapon to entrap cheating husbands. And possibly non-cheating ones as well.

'Is this the guy?' Dora asked, picking up the photo that was resting in the middle of the table.

'Yep. That's him.'

'He's handsome.'

Jessie had thought so too. Far better looking than the other creeps she'd had to flirt with. And younger. In his thirties instead of forties or fifties. But she had no doubts about the type of man he was.

'Handsome is as handsome does, Dora. He's married with two little kids, yet he spends every Friday night at a bar in town, drinking till all hours of the night.'

'But lots of men drink on a Friday night.'

'I doubt he's just drinking. The particular city bar he frequents is a well-known pick-up joint,' Jessie pointed out drily.

'You could say that about any bar.'

'Look, the wife says this behaviour is out of character with her husband. She says he's changed towards her. She's convinced he's being unfaithful to her and wants to know the truth.'

'Doesn't sound like compelling evidence of adultery to me. She might wish she hadn't started this.'

'What do you mean?'

'You know, Jessie, I've never thought it was very fair on the men in question, sending a girl like you to flirt with them. This man might not have been unfaithful at all. Maybe he's just working very hard and having an extra drink or two at the end of the week to relax. Then you come along tonight and give him the eye, and he might do something he wouldn't normally do, something he might regret.'

Jessie had to laugh. Dora made her sound like some kind of siren. Irresistible she was not! Just ask all the male bosses who hadn't given her a job this past year.

No, poor Dora didn't know what she was talking about, especially regarding tonight's target. Still, Dora *was* sixty-six years old. In her day, maybe more men had more honour.

'Trust me, Dora. By the time wives go to see Jack Keegan and spend the kind of money he asks for, then there really isn't any doubt over their husbands' philandering. All they're looking for is proof to show the lawyers. Our Mr Curtis Marshall here,' she said, taking his photo out of Dora's hand and looking down into his baby-blue eyes, 'is not some poor, hard-working, misunderstood hubby. He's been playing out of his patch and he's about to get caught! Now I really must get going,' she said as she slid the photo in a zippered side-section of her bag. 'I'll just go check on Emily before I leave.'

Jessie tiptoed into the bedroom, where a sound-asleep Emily had kicked off her bedclothes. The evening was quite warm, so Jessie switched the overhead ceiling fan on to the slow setting, then pulled the top sheet up around Emily and tucked her in. Emily had not long given up her cot for a single bed and looked such a dot in the larger bed.

Pressing a kiss to her temple, Jessie straightened before just standing there and staring down at her daughter.

Her heart filled with love as it always did when she looked down upon her child.

That was what had surprised Jessie the most when she'd become a mother. The instant and totally unconditional love which had consumed her from the moment she'd held her baby in her arms.

Had her own mother felt like that when she'd had her?

Jessie didn't think so. She suspected that any love her mother had had for her had been overshadowed by shame.

Jessie pushed this distressing thought aside and bent to stroke Emily's dark curls back from her forehead before planting another gentle kiss on her daughter's cheek.

'Sleep tight, sweetie,' she whispered. 'Mummy won't be long.

'Thank you so much for staying here and minding

her, Dora,' Jessie said on returning to the combined kitchen and living room.

'My pleasure,' Dora said, already settled on the sofa in front of the television.

'You know where the tea and biscuits are.'

'I'll be fine. There's a good movie on tonight at eight-thirty. That's only ten minutes off. You'd better get going. And for Pete's sake, take a taxi home after you're finished. It's too dangerous on the train late at night, especially on a Friday night.'

'Hopefully, I won't be too late.'

Jessie didn't want to waste any of the travel expenses Jack had given her. She wanted to make as much profit out of this rotten evening as she could. Why waste thirty dollars on a cab?

'Jessie Denton,' Dora said sternly. 'You promise me you'll take a taxi home.'

Jessie gave her a narrow-eyed look from under her long lashes. 'I will if I need to, Dora.'

'You can be very stubborn, do you know that?'

Jessie grinned. 'Yep. But you love me just the same. Take care.' And, giving Dora a peck on the cheek, she swept up her bag and headed for the door.

CHAPTER TWO

KANE sat at the bar, nursing a double Scotch, and pondering the perversities of life.

He still could not believe what his brother had just told him: that he was miserable in his marriage and that he spent every Friday night drinking here at this bar instead of going home to his wife and children. Curtis even confessed to going into the office on the weekend sometimes to escape the tension and arguments at home.

Kane could not have been more shocked. There he'd been these past few years, envying Curtis for his choice of wife, his two gorgeous children and his seemingly perfect family!

The truth, it seemed, was a far cry from the fantasy world Kane had woven around his twin brother's home life. Apparently, Lisa was far from content with being a stay-at-home mum. She was bored and lonely for adult company during the day. On top of that, two-year-old Joshua had turned into a right terror this past year. Four-year-old Cathy threw tantrums all the time and wouldn't go to bed at night. Lisa could not cope and their sex life had been reduced to zero.

Curtis, who was never at his best at the art of communication, had started staying away from home more and more, and Lisa was now giving him the silent treatment.

He was terrified she was thinking of leaving him and taking the kids with her. Which had prompted his call of desperation to his brother tonight.

Kane, who'd been working late at the office, solving the problem of a defecting designer, had come running to the rescue—as he always did when his twin brother was hurt or threatened in any way. He'd been coming to Curtis's rescue since they were toddlers.

'I love my family and don't want to lose them,' Curtis had cried into his beer ten minutes earlier. 'Tell me what to do, Kane. You're the man with all the solutions. Tell me what to do!'

Kane had rolled his eyes at this. OK, he could understand why Curtis thought he could wave a magic wand and fix his problems with a few, well-chosen words. He *had* made a fortune teaching people how to be successful in getting what they wanted out of their working life. His motivational seminars drew huge crowds. His fee as an after-dinner speaker was outrageous. His best-selling book, *Winning At Work*, had been picked up in most countries overseas.

Earlier this year he'd gone on a whirlwind tour in the US to promote the book's release, and sales there had been stupendous.

His hectic schedule in America had drained him, however, both physically and emotionally, and since his return he'd cut back considerably on his speaking engagements. He'd been thinking of taking a long holiday when his friend Harry Wilde had asked him to look after his small but very successful advertising agency during December whilst he went on a cruise with his wife and kids.

Kane had jumped at the chance. A change was as good as a holiday. And he was really enjoying the challenge. It had been interesting to see if his theories could be applied to any management job. So far, so good.

Unfortunately, his strategies for success in the professional world didn't necessarily translate into success in one's personal life. His own, especially. With one failed marriage behind him and no new relationship in sight, he was possibly not the best man to give his brother marital advice.

But he knew one thing. You never solved any problem by sitting at a bar, downing one beer after another. You certainly never solved anything, running away from life.

Of course, that had always been Curtis's nature, to take the easiest course, to run away from trouble. He'd always been the shy twin. The less assertive twin. The one who needed protecting. Although just as intelligent, Curtis had never had Kane's confidence, or drive, or ambition. His choice to become an accountant had not surprised Kane.

Still, Kane understood that it could not have been easy being *his* twin brother. He knew he could be a hard act to follow, with his I-can-do-anything personality.

But it was high time Curtis stood up and faced life head-on, along with his responsibilities. He had a lovely wife and two great kids who were having a hard time for whatever reason and really needed him. Regardless of what a lot of those new relationship gurus touted, Kane believed a husband was supposed to be the head of his family. The rock. The person they could always count on.

Curtis was acting like a coward.

Not that Kane said that. Rule one in his advice to management executives was never to criticise or put down their staff or their colleagues. Praise and encouragement worked much better than pointing out an individual's shortcomings.

In light of that theory, Kane had delivered Curtis one of his best motivational lectures ever, telling his brother what a great bloke he was. A great brother, a great son, a great husband and a great father. He even threw in that Curtis was a great accountant. Didn't he do his brother's highly complicated tax return each year?

Kane reassured Curtis that his wife loved him and no way would she ever leave him.

Unless she thought he didn't love her back. Which Lisa *had* to be thinking, Kane reckoned.

At this point he sent his brother off home to tell his wife that he loved her to death and that he was sorry that he hadn't been there for her when she needed him. He was to vow passionately that he would be in future, and what could he do to help?

'And when Lisa falls, weeping, into your arms,' Kane had added, 'whip her into bed and make love to her as you obviously haven't made love to her in a long time!'

When Curtis still hesitated, Kane also promised to

drop over the next day to give his brother some moral support, and to provide some more proactive suggestions which would make his wife and kids a lot happier.

Hopefully, by then, he could think of some.

One divorce in their family was more than enough! Their parents would have a fit if Curtis and Lisa broke up as well.

Kane shook his head and swirled his drink, staring down into the pale amber depths and wondering just why he'd married Natalie in the first place. For a guy who was supposed to be smart, he'd been very dumb that time. Their marriage had been doomed from the start.

'Hi, honey.'

Kane's head whipped around to find a very good-looking blonde sliding seductively onto the bar stool next to him. Everything she had—and there was plenty of it—was on display. For a split-second, Kane felt his male hormones rumble a bit. Till he looked into her eyes.

They were pretty enough, but empty. Kane could never stay interested in women with empty eyes.

Natalie had had intelligent eyes.

Pity she hadn't wanted children.

'You look as if you could do with some company,' the blonde added before curling her finger at the barman and ordering herself a glass of champagne.

'Bad week?' she directed back at Kane.

'Nope. Good week. Not so great an evening,' he replied, still thinking of his brother's problems.

'Loneliness is lousy,' she said.

'I'm not lonely,' he refuted. 'Just alone.'

'Not any more.'

'Maybe I want to be alone.'

'No one *wants* to be alone, lover.'

The blonde's words struck home. She was right. No one did. Him included. But divorce—even an amicable one—made a man wary. It had been fifteen months since he'd separated from Natalie, three months since their divorce had become final. And he still hadn't found anyone new. He hadn't even succumbed to the many offers he'd had for one-night stands.

Women were always letting him know they were available for the night, or a weekend, or whatever. But he just wasn't interested in that kind of encounter any more. He'd been hoping to find what he thought Curtis had. A woman who wasn't wrapped up in her career. A woman who was happy to put her job aside for a few years at least to become a career wife, and mother.

Now he wasn't so sure if that creature existed. The sort of women he found attractive were invariably involved with their jobs. They were smart, sassy, sexy girls who worked hard and played hard. They didn't want to become housewives and mothers.

'Come on, lighten up a bit,' the blonde said. 'Get yourself another drink, for pity's sake. That one's history.'

Kane knew he probably shouldn't. He hadn't had anything to eat tonight and the whisky was going straight to his head. He wasn't interested in the blonde, but neither did he want to go home to an empty house. He'd have one more drink with her, then make his excuses and go find a place in town to eat.

CHAPTER THREE

THE bar Curtis Marshall frequented every Friday
night was called the Cellar, so Jessie shouldn't have
been surprised to find that it was downstairs from
street level. Narrow, steep stairs. Stairs which made
her walk oh, so carefully in her four-inch-high heels.
The last thing she wanted was to fall flat on her face.

The music reached her ears only seconds before
the smoke.

Jazz.

Not Jessie's favourite form of music. But what did
it matter? She wasn't there to enjoy herself. She was
there to do a job.

The bouncer standing by the open door gave her
the once-over as she slowly negotiated the last few
steps.

'Very nice,' he muttered as she walked past him.

She didn't answer. She straightened her shoulders
and moved further into the smoke haze, her eyes
slowly becoming accustomed to the dimmer lighting
as they scanned the not-so-crowded room. Nine
o'clock, she reasoned, was between times. Most of
the Friday after-work drinkers had departed, and the
serious weekend party animals had not yet arrived.

She'd never been to this particular bar before.
She'd never heard of it. It was Jack who'd informed
her that it had a reputation as a pick-up joint.

The décor was nineteen-twenties speak-easy style, with lots of wood and leather and brass. Booths lined the walls, with tables and chairs filling every other available space. The band occupied one corner, with a very small dance floor in front of it.

The bar itself was against the far wall, semicircular in shape, graced by a dozen or so wooden-based, leather-topped stools. A long mirror ran along the back behind the bottle shelves, which gave Jessie reflected glimpses of the faces of people sitting at the bar.

There were only half a dozen.

She recognised her target straight away. He was sitting in the middle, with a blonde sitting next to him on his left. There were several vacant stools to his right. As Jessie stood there, watching them, she saw the blonde lean over and say something to him. He motioned to the barman, who came over, temporarily blocking Jessie's view of the target's face in the mirror.

Had the blonde asked him to buy her a drink? Was he right at this moment doing exactly what his wife suspected him of?

Jessie realised with a rush of relief that maybe she wouldn't have to flirt with the creep after all. If she got over there right now, she could collect evidence of his chatting up some other woman without having to belittle herself.

Jessie's heart pounded as she headed for the bar, nerves cramping her stomach. She still hated doing this, even second-hand.

Think of the money, she told herself as she slid up

on the vacant stool two to the right of the target. *Think of Emily's beautiful, beaming face on Christmas morning when she finds that Santa has brought her exactly what she asked for.*

The self-lecture helped a little. Some composure returned by the time Jessie placed her bag down on the polished wooden bar-top. Very casually she extracted the mobile phone, pretended to check her text messages, turned on the video then put it down in a position which would catch what was going on to her left, both visually and verbally.

'Thanks,' the blonde purred when the barman put a glass of champagne in front of her. 'So what will we drink to, handsome?'

When the barman moved away, Jessie was able to watch the target's face again in the mirror behind the bar.

There was no doubt he *was* handsome, more handsome than in his photograph. More mature-looking, too. Maybe that photo in her bag was a couple of years old, because his hair was different as well. Not different in colour. It was still a mid-brown. But in place of the longer waves and lock flopping across his forehead was a short-back-and-sides look, with spikes on top.

The style brought his blue eyes more into focus.

That was another thing that looked different. His eyes. In the photo they'd seemed a baby-blue, with a dreamy expression. In reality, his eyes were an icy blue. And not soft at all.

They glittered as he smiled wryly and swirled the

remains of his drink. He hadn't noticed her arrival as yet.

'To marriage,' he said, and lifted his glass in a toast.

'*Marriage!*' the blonde scorned. 'That's one seriously out-of-date institution. I'd rather drink to divorce.'

'Divorce is a blight on our society,' he said sharply. 'I won't drink to divorce.'

'Sex, then. Let's drink to sex.' And she slid her glass against his in a very suggestive fashion.

Jessie, who'd stayed surreptitiously watching him in the mirror behind the bar, saw his head turn slowly towards the blonde, a drily amused expression on his face.

'Sweetheart, I think you've picked the wrong guy to share a drink with. I'm sorry if I've given you the wrong impression, but I'm not in the market for what you're looking for tonight.'

Jessie almost fell off her stool. What was this? A man with some honour? Had Dora been right about Mr Marshall after all?

'You sure?' the blonde persisted with a sultry smile playing on her red-painted mouth.

'Positive.'

'Your loss, lover,' she said and, taking her glass of champagne, slid off her stool and sashayed over to sit at a table close to the band. She wasn't by herself for more than ten seconds, before a guy who'd been sitting further down the bar had taken *his* beer with him to join her.

Jessie glanced back into the mirror to find that her

target had finally noticed her presence, and was staring at her. When their eyes connected in the glass her heart reacted in a way which it hadn't in years. It actually jumped, then fluttered, then flipped right over.

Her eyes remained locked with his for longer than was wise, her brain screaming at her to look away, but her body took absolutely no notice.

Suddenly a man plonked himself down on the vacant stool that separated them, snapping her back to reality.

'Haven't seen you in here before, gorgeous,' the interloper said in slurred tones, his beery breath wafting over her. 'Can I buy you a drink?'

He was about forty, a very short, very drunk weasel of a man in a cheap, ill-fitting business suit that bore no resemblance to the magnificently tailored Italian number the target was wearing.

'No, thanks,' Jessie said stiffly. 'I like to buy my own drinks.'

'One of them feminists, eh? That's all right by me. Cheaper this way.'

'I also like to drink alone,' she added sharply.

The drunk laughed. 'A sexy piece like you shouldn't be doing anything alone. What's the matter, honey? Last guy do you wrong? Or ain't I young enough for you? Trust me. I've still got it where it counts. Here, let me show you...'

He was actually fumbling with his fly when two big hands grabbed him and literally lifted him off the stool.

'Let *me* show *you* something, buster,' the target said. 'The door!'

Jessie watched, open-mouthed, as her unexpected knight in shining armour carried the drunk over to where the bouncer was frowning at them both. Words were exchanged after which the bouncer escorted the weasel up the stairs personally whilst Jessie's champion headed back for the bar.

She found herself admiring more than his handsome face this time.

There was the way his broad shoulders filled out his expensive suit. The way he'd just handled the situation. And the way he was smiling at her.

That smile was pure dynamite. As well as something else that wasn't at all pure.

Suddenly, Jessie was catapulted back to earlier that evening when she'd been thinking about how pleasurable it would be to be in some gorgeous man's arms.

She started thinking about how pleasurable it would be to be in *this* man's arms. He was definitely gorgeous.

But he was also married. And sitting back down, she realised breathlessly, *not* on his old stool but the one right next to hers, the one the drunk had occupied.

Dora's words came back to haunt her, the ones that she'd said about how it wasn't fair to send someone like her to flirt; that she might tempt her target tonight to do something he might regret.

But logic argued against this concern. That blonde

had been very attractive. If he was going to be tempted, then why hadn't *she* tempted him?

Maybe he doesn't go for blondes, came back another voice, just as logical. Maybe he likes leggy women with wild black hair. Maybe he likes women who aren't quite so obvious.

There were many reasons why men were attracted to one woman over another.

And he *was* attracted to her. She could see it in his eyes. And in that heart-stopping smile.

'Th…thank you,' she stammered.

'You can buy me another Scotch and soda in gratitude if you like,' he said, and downed what was left of his drink. 'Unless you really meant what you said about preferring to drink alone.' And he smiled at her again.

Jessie's heart ground to a shuddering halt.

Get out of here now, girl, her conscience warned. This guy is not just dynamite, he's downright dangerous!

'I was just trying to get rid of him,' she heard herself saying.

'I was hoping that might be the case. So what can I get you? After all, a gentleman doesn't really expect a lady to buy his drinks for him.'

Jessie swallowed. What are you doing, girl? Stop looking at him that way. Stop it right now!

I'm just doing my job, she tried telling herself. This is what I get paid for. Flirting with my target. Seeing what kind of man he is.

Yes, but you're not supposed to be enjoying it!

'Just a diet cola, thanks.'

His straight brows lifted in the middle. 'You come into a bar for a diet cola? Now, that's a strange thing to do. You can get one of those from a vending machine.'

'Maybe I came in looking for some company,' she said leadingly, and hoped like hell he'd put his foot in his mouth right away so she could get out of there.

'I can't imagine a girl like you would have to do that too often. You must have men asking you out all the time.'

Actually, she did. But no one she'd give the time of day to. The men who asked her out had her tagged as one of two types: waitressing slut or single-mother-and-desperate, depending on when and where they met her.

Either way, Jessie always knew exactly what they wanted from her, and it wasn't witty conversation.

She always said no to their invitations.

One-night stands held no appeal for her. Sex of any kind had held no appeal for her.

Till tonight...

'Give me another Scotch and soda,' the target directed to the barman. 'And get the lady a Bacardi and cola. *Diet* cola,' he added with a quick grin her way.

She swallowed. 'What if I don't like Bacardi and cola?'

'Come, now, you and I both know that the amount of Bacardi they put in drinks in places like this is barely detectable. All you'll taste is the cola.'

'True,' she agreed.

'So was that other chap right?' he went on whilst

the barman busied himself with their drinks. 'Did your last boyfriend do you wrong? Is that why you're all alone tonight?'

She shrugged. 'Something like that.'

'Aah. A woman of mystery and intrigue. I like that. It makes for a change.'

'A change from what?'

'From women who launch into their life story as soon as you meet them.'

'Does that happen to you often?'

'Too often.'

'Did the blonde over there do that?'

'Actually, no. But then, she had other things on her mind tonight. Looks as if she finally hit the jackpot.'

Jessie flicked a glance over at where the blonde was now leaving with the man who'd joined her earlier. It didn't take a genius to guess that they were going back to her place. Or his. Or maybe even a hotel. There were several within easy walking distance of this bar.

'Most men would have jumped at the chance,' she remarked.

'I'm not most men.'

'Yes. Yes, I can see that.'

Their drinks came, giving Jessie a breather from the tension that was gripping her chest. As cool as she was sounding on the outside, inside she was seriously rattled. She liked this man. *More* than liked. She found him fascinating. And sexy. Oh, so sexy.

'What about you?' she asked, deciding to deflect the conversation on to him, make him admit he was married. Anything to lessen her worry over where their conversation might lead.

'What about me?' he returned before taking a deep swallow of his drink.

'Did your last girlfriend do *you* wrong? Is that why *you're* alone here tonight?'

He drank some more whilst he gave her question some thought. Suspense built in Jessie till she wanted to scream at him to just confess the truth. That *he* was the one in the wrong here. Regardless of how stressed he might feel with life, he should be at home with his wife and kids. She'd heard him say that divorce was a blight on society. Did he want to find himself in the middle of one?

Finally, he looked up and slanted a smile over at her. 'You know what? I'm going to take a leaf out of your book. No talking about past relationships tonight. I think sometimes I talk way too much. Come on,' he pronounced and put his drink down. 'The music's changed to something decent. Let's dance.'

Jessie stiffened, then gulped down a huge mouthful of Bacardi and cola. 'Dance?' she choked out.

He was already off his stool, already holding out his hand towards her.

'Please don't say no,' he said softly. 'It's just a dance. Mind the lady's bag, will you?' he asked the barman. 'Better put your cellphone away as well. You don't want a natty little number like that to get swiped.'

She did hesitate, she was sure she did. But within moments she'd put the phone away and was placing her hand in his and letting him lead her over to that minute dance floor.

It *is* only dancing, she told herself as he pulled her into his arms.

The trouble was, there was dancing…and dancing.

This was slow dancing. Sensual dancing. Sexy dancing. Bodies pressed so close together that she had no choice but to wind her arms up around his neck. Her breasts lifted, rubbing against the well-muscled wall of his chest. His hands moved restlessly up and down her spine till one settled in the small of her back, the other moving lower. The heat in his palms burned through the thin material of her dress, branding her. Her heartbeat quickened. The entire surface of her skin flushed with her own internal heat. She felt light-headed. Excited. Aroused.

And she wasn't the only one. She could feel his arousal as it rose between them.

When her fingertips tapped an agitated tattoo on the nape of his neck, he stopped, pulled back slightly and stared down into her eyes.

'Would you believe me if I told you that I haven't done anything like this in a long, long time?' he murmured, his voice low and thick.

'Done what?' she replied shakily.

'Picked a girl up in a bar and within no time asked her to go to a hotel with me?'

She stopped breathing. Stopped thinking. Her world had tipped on its axis and she felt every ounce of her self-control slipping. A voice was tempting her to blindly say yes. Yes, to anything he wanted. She had never in her life felt what she was feeling at this moment. Not even with Lyall.

This was something else, something far more powerful and infinitely more dangerous.

'Will you?' he said, and his smouldering gaze searched hers.

She didn't say a word. But her eyes must have told him something.

'No names,' he murmured. 'Not yet. Not till afterwards. I don't want to say anything that might spoil what we're sharing at this moment. Because I have never felt anything quite like it before. Tell me it's the same for you. Admit it. Say you want me as badly as I want you.'

She couldn't say it. But every fibre of her female body compelled her to cling to him, betraying her cravings with her body language.

'You do talk too much,' she whispered at last.

His lungs expelled a shuddering sigh. Of relief? Or was he trying to dispel some of the sexual tension that was gripping them both?

'Then you *will* come with me,' he said. 'Now. Straight away.'

They weren't questions, but orders.

He would be an incredible lover, she realised. Knowing. Dominating. Demanding. The kind she had used to fantasise about. And which she suddenly craved.

'I…I have to go to the ladies' first,' she blurted out, desperate to get away from him. Once some distance broke the spell he was casting over her, she would recover her sanity and escape.

'I suppose I could do with a visit to the gents' as well. I'll meet you back at the bar.'

She didn't meet him back at the bar. She spent less than twenty seconds in the ladies' before dashing back to the bar, collecting her bag from the barman and bolting for the exit. She ran all the way to Wynyard Station, where she jumped on the first train heading north.

It was only half an hour since she'd walked into that bar. But it felt like a lifetime.

CHAPTER FOUR

'THE phone's ringing, Mummy.' Emily tugged at Jessie's jeans. 'Mummy, are you listening to me? The phone's ringing.'

'What? Oh, yes. Thanks, sweetie.'

Jessie dropped the wet T-shirt she was holding back into the clothes basket and ran across the yard towards her back door.

Goodness knew who it would be. She'd already rung Jack first thing this morning to put in a verbal report about last night, petrified at the time that he'd know she was lying.

She'd made up her mind overnight to give Mr Marshall the benefit of the doubt and only tell Jack about the incident with the blonde, and not the conversation that had happened later. She'd already wiped that part off the video as well.

But no sooner had she told him that she'd witnessed the target turning down a proposition from an attractive blonde than Jack had stunned her by saying he wasn't surprised, that the wife herself had rung that morning in a panic to say that he could keep the money she'd already paid, but that she didn't want her husband followed any more. It had all been a mistake and a misunderstanding. He'd come home last night and explained everything and she was very happy.

At which point Jack had added smarmily that he could guess what had happened in the Marshall household last night.

'I can always tell,' he'd joked. 'The wives' voices have a certain sound about them. A combination of coyness and confidence. Our Mr Marshall really came good, I'd say. Like to have been a fly on their bedroom wall last night, I can tell you.'

That image had stayed with Jessie all morning—of her actually being a fly on that bedroom wall, watching whilst the man she'd danced with last night, the man who'd wanted her so desperately, was making love to his wife.

Jessie knew it was wicked of her to feel jealousy over a husband making love to his wife. Wicked to wish she'd been the one in his bed. Wicked, wicked, wicked!

But she couldn't seem to stop her thoughts, or her feelings. She'd hardly slept a wink all night.

Now, as she dashed inside to the strident sound of the phone, she could still see the desire in his eyes, hear the passion in his voice, feel the need of his body pressed up against hers.

Had he been telling the truth when he said this was a one-off experience? That he'd never done or felt anything like that before?

She was inclined to believe him. Possibly, he'd been more intoxicated than he looked. Or he'd been too long without sex. Silly to believe that there'd been something special between them, right from the first moment their eyes had connected.

That was the romantic in her talking. Men thought

differently to women, especially about sex. All she'd been to him was a potential one-night stand.

Maybe, after he discovered she'd done a flit, he'd been relieved. Maybe he'd rushed home in a fit of guilt and shame and genuinely made things up with his wife. Maybe he hadn't simply used the desire Jessie had engendered in him to make love to a woman he didn't feel excited by any more.

But why would he do that? For his children's sake?

Perhaps. Christmas was coming up soon. A family should be together at Christmas. He did hate divorce. She'd heard him say so. And he'd toasted marriage.

Clearly, his marriage mattered to him.

She had to stop thinking about him, Jessie decided as she snatched the receiver down off the kitchen wall. Whatever happened last night, it was over and done with. She would never see the man again. End of story. *Finis!*

'Yes,' she answered breathlessly into the phone.

'Jessie Denton?'

'Speaking.'

'It's Nicholas Hanks here, Jessie, from Adstaff.'

'Pardon? Who?' And then the penny dropped. 'Oh, yes, Adstaff. The employment agency. Sorry, it's been a while since I heard from you.'

'True, but, as I explained to you earlier this year, the market for graphic artists isn't very buoyant at the moment. Still, something came up yesterday and I thought of you immediately.'

'Really? Why me, especially?' Any initial jolt of excitement was tempered by her experiences in the past. Recruitment people were, by nature, optimists. You had to take what they said with a grain of salt sometimes.

'This particular advertising agency wants someone who can start straight away,' the recruiter rattled on. 'They don't want to interview anyone who's currently employed with another agency.'

Jessie's heart sank. There had to be dozens of unemployed graphic artists in Sydney. Once again, the odds of her securing this much-sought-after job was minimal.

'So which agency is it?' she asked, refusing to get her hopes up.

'*Wild Ideas.*'

'Oh!' Jessie groaned. 'I'd *love* to work for them.'

Her, and just about every other graphic artist in Sydney. Wild Ideas was only small compared to some advertising agencies. But it was innovative and very successful. Run by advertising pin-up boy Harry Wilde, it had a reputation for promoting any graphic artist with flair to the position of creative designer, rather than head-hunting them from other agencies.

'Yes, I thought you might,' came the drily amused reply. 'You have an interview there at ten o'clock Monday morning.'

'Gosh, that soon.' She'd have to ring the restaurant. Fortunately, Monday was their least busy day; if she rang early, they'd be able to call in one of the casuals, no trouble.

'Can you start straight away, if you have to?'

'Too right I can. But let's be honest…Nicholas, wasn't it…what are the odds of that happening?'

'Actually, you have an even-money chance. We sent over the CVs of several people on our books yesterday afternoon and they've already whittled them down to two. You're one of those two. Apparently, they're keen to fill this position, post-haste, and don't want to waste time interviewing all the would-bes if there are could-bes. I remember your portfolio very well, Jessie, so I know you have the talent required. And you interview very well. Frankly, I was very surprised you weren't snapped up for that art job I sent you along for earlier on in the year.'

Jessie sighed. 'I wasn't surprised. Regardless of what they say, some employers are dead against hiring a single mother. They don't say so straight out, but underneath they worry that you'll want time off when your kid's sick or something. I'm sure that's been part of my problem all along.'

'Jessie, your single-mother status is clearly stated on your résumé, which Wild Ideas has already seen. Yet they still specifically asked for you. Clearly, your being a single mum didn't deter them, did it? You do have your little girl in full-time care, don't you?'

'Yes. But…'

'But nothing. Your circumstances are no different from those of any other working mum, be they single or married. What will count with Wild Ideas is your creative talent, your professional attitude and your reliability. Impress them on those three levels and I feel confident that this job will be yours.'

Jessie had to struggle to control the stirrings of excitement. No way could she afford to get carried away with false optimism. She'd been there, done that, and at the end of the day was always bitterly disappointed.

'You talk as if I'm the only one going for this job,' she pointed out. 'There is another applicant, isn't there?'

'Er—yes,' came the rather reluctant reply.

'Well, presumably this person is just as well-qualified for this job as I am.'

'Mmm. Yes. And no.'

'Meaning what?'

'Look, it would be very unprofessional of me to say anything negative about the other applicant. She is a client of our agency as well.'

She. It was a woman.

'But let me give you a hint when it comes to what you wear for your interview. Nothing too bright or too way-out or too overtly sexy.'

Jessie was taken aback. 'But I never dress like that. You've met me. I'm a very conservative dresser.'

'Yes, but you might have thought that going for a job at Wild Ideas required you to present a certain…image. Trust me when I tell you that your chances of being employed there will be greatly enhanced if you dress very simply.'

'You mean, in a suit or something?'

'That might be overkill, under the circumstances. I would suggest something smart, but casual.'

'Would jeans be too casual? I have some really nice jeans. Not ones with frayed holes in them. They're dark blue and very smart. I could wear them with a white shirt and a jacket.'

'Sounds perfect.'

'And I'll put my hair up. Down, it can look a bit wild. What about make-up? Should I wear make-up?'

'Not too much.'

'Right.' Jessie speculated that the other applicant was possibly a flashy female, who tried to trade on her sex appeal. Not an uncommon event in the advertising world. Perhaps with Harry Wilde now being a married man instead of a playboy, he preferred to play it safe over who he hired these days. Maybe Nicholas was subtly advising her that the *femme fatale* type would not be looked upon favourably.

'Is there anything else I should know?' she asked.

'No. Just be your usual honest and open self and I'm sure everything will work out.'

'You've been very kind. Thank you.'

'My pleasure. I'm only sorry I haven't been able to find you a job sooner.'

'I haven't got *this* job yet.'

'You will.'

Jessie wished she could share his supreme confidence, but life had taught her not to count her chickens before they hatched.

'Have to go, Jessie. There's someone else on the line. Good luck on Monday.' And he hung up.

Jessie hung up as well, only then thinking of Emily still out in the back yard all by herself.

Her heart started thudding as a mother's heart always did when she realised she'd taken her eyes off her child for a few seconds too long.

Not that Emily was the sort of child who got herself into trouble. She was careful, and a thinker. Her pleasures were quiet ones. She wasn't a climber. Neither did she do silly things. She was absolutely *nothing* like her father. She was a hundred per cent smarter, for starters.

Still, when Jessie hurried back outside into the yard, she was very relieved to see Emily was where she spent most of her time, playing under the large fig tree in the corner. It was her cubby house, with the sections between the huge roots making perfect pretend rooms. Emily could happily play there for hours.

Her daughter had a wonderful imagination. Jessie had been the same as a child. Maybe it was an only-child thing. Or an inherited talent. Or a bit of both.

Whatever, the Denton girls loved being creative.

Jessie realised then that she wanted that job at Wild Ideas, not just for the money, but also for herself. Being a waitress had been a good stopgap, but she didn't want to do it for the rest of her life. She wanted to use her mind. She wanted the challenges—and the excitement—of the advertising world.

'Mummy, who rang our phone? Was it Dora?'

Jessie, who'd finished hanging out the washing, bent down and swept her daughter up into her arms. It was time for lunch.

'No, sweetie, not Dora. It was a man.'

Emily blinked. 'A nice man?'

'Very nice.'

'Is he going to be your boyfriend, Mummy?'

'What? Oh, no. Heavens, no! He's just a man who finds people jobs. It looks as if he might have found Mummy a job as a graphic artist. I have to go for an interview on Monday. If I get it, I'll earn a lot more money and I'll be able to buy you lots of pretty things.'

Emily didn't seem as impressed with this news as Jessie would have expected. She was frowning.

'Why don't you have a boyfriend, Mummy? You're very pretty.'

Jessie felt herself blushing. 'I…I just haven't met any man I liked enough to have as a boyfriend.'

Even as she said the words, a pair of ice-blue eyes popped into her mind, along with a charismatic smile. Her heart lurched at the memory of how close she'd come to making the same mistake her mother had made. Brother, she'd got out of that bar just in time.

'I have *you*, sweetie,' Jessie said, giving her daughter a squeeze. 'I don't need anyone or anything else.'

Which was the biggest lie Jessie had told her daughter since she'd said she liked being a waitress. Because last night's experience showed her she *did* need something else sometimes, didn't she? She needed to feel like a woman occasionally, not just a mother. She needed to have a man's arms around her once more. She needed some release from the frustration she could feel building up inside her.

Some day, she would have to find an outlet for those needs. A man, obviously. A boyfriend, as Emily suggested.

But who?

Those blue eyes jumped back into her mind.

Well, obviously not him. He was off limits. A married man.

If only she could get this job. That would bring a whole new circle of males into her world.

OK, so lots of guys in the advertising world were gay. But some weren't. Surely there had to be the right kind of boyfriend out there for her. Someone attractive and intelligent. Someone single—and a good lover.

Of course, attractive, intelligent *single* men who were good lovers were invariably full of themselves, and unwilling to commit. There would be no real future in such a relationship. She'd have to be careful not to fall for the guy. Or to start hoping for more than such a man could give.

Jessie sighed. Did she honestly need such complications in her life? Wouldn't it be better if she just went along the way she was, being a celibate single mum?

Men were trouble. Always had been. Always would be. She was much better off without one in her life. Emily was happy. *She* was happy. She'd be even happier if she got this job on Monday.

Feeling frustrated was just a temporary thing. She'd get over it. One day.

Jessie sighed again.

'Why are you always sighing today, Mummy?' Emily asked. 'Are you tired?'

'A little, sweetie.'

'Why don't you have a cup of coffee? You always do that when you're tired.'

Jessie looked into her daughter's beautiful

brown eyes and laughed. 'You know me very well, don't you?'

'Yes, Mummy,' she said in that strangely grown-up voice she used sometimes. 'I do. Oh, I can hear Dora's car! Let's go and tell her about your new job.'

'I haven't got it yet, Emily. It's only an interview.'

'You'll get it, Mummy,' she said with all the naïve confidence of a four-year-old. 'You will get the job.'

CHAPTER FIVE

THE offices of Wild Ideas were in north Sydney, on the third floor of an office block not far from North Sydney Station. A bonus for Jessie, who didn't own a car.

She arrived in the foyer of the building early, dressed in her best stone-washed jeans and a freshly starched white shirt, turned up at the collar. She carried a lightweight black jacket—in case the air-conditioning inside was brutal—as well as a black briefcase. Her shoes were sensible black pumps, well-worn but polished that morning till they shone.

Her hair was pulled back tightly and secured at the nape of her neck with a black and white printed scarf she'd borrowed from Dora. Her make-up was on the neutral side, especially around her eyes and on her mouth. The only jewelry she wore were small silver cross earrings. Plus her watch. She'd be lost without her watch.

She glanced at it now. Still only twenty-five minutes to ten. She wasn't going up to Wild Ideas yet. Only desperates arrived that early. Instead she headed for the powder room, where she spent a few minutes checking that she didn't look like a *femme fatale*.

Actually, her appearance would be considered *very* conservative in advertising circles. But she'd never

been a flashy dresser, even when she could afford
to be.

Finally, she gave in to her pounding heart and rode
the lift up to the third floor. It had been some months
since she'd been for a job interview and she felt sick
with nerves and tension. Not because she didn't think
she could do the job. Jessie had never been lacking
in confidence in her own abilities. But after being
knocked back as often as she had, she'd begun to
wonder if anyone would ever see what she had to
offer.

Still, this chance was the best she'd had so far. *An
even-money chance.*

As Jessie exited the lift on the third floor, she wondered if the other applicant was in there now, being
interviewed, impressing the boss so much that he
wouldn't even bother to see her. Maybe the receptionist would say 'Thank you very much but the job's
already taken'.

Jessie took a deep breath and told herself not to
be so silly. Or so negative. Harry Wilde had obviously liked her résumé. Surely, he'd have the de-
cency to give her an interview.

The reception area of Wild Ideas fitted its image.
Modern and colourful, with crisp, clean lines and furniture. Red-painted walls, covered in advertising
posters. Black tiled floor. Very shiny. The sofas were
in cream leather, the desk and coffee-tables made of
blond wood.

The receptionist was blond as well, but not overly
glamorous or overly beautiful. Possibly thirty, she

wore a neat black suit and a nice smile—not the sort of smile used before delivering bad news.

'Hello,' she said brightly when Jessie walked in. 'You'll be Jessie Denton.'

'Yes, that's right,' Jessie replied, her palms still distinctly sweaty. 'I'm a bit early.'

'Better than being late. Or not turning up at all,' the blonde added ruefully. 'I'll just give Karen a ring to let her know you've arrived. Karen's Mr Wilde's PA,' she explained. 'Just take a seat over there for a sec.' And she motioned towards one of the seats that lined the waiting-room walls.

'Jessie Denton's here, Karen,' she heard the receptionist say quietly into the phone. 'OK… Yes, I'll tell her.'

By the time she looked up, Jessie had sat down, leant back and crossed her legs, doing her best to appear cool and confident. Inside, she was a bundle of nerves.

'Mr Marshall hasn't finished with the other applicant yet,' the receptionist informed her. 'But he won't be long.'

'Mr *Marshall*?' Jessie choked out, her legs uncrossing as she jerked forward on the seat. 'But…but…'

'Mr Wilde is overseas at the moment,' the receptionist cut into Jessie's stammering, and before she could recover from her shock. 'Mr Marshall is in charge while he's away.'

'Oh. I see. Right.' Jessie took a deep breath and leant back again, exhaling slowly. Crazy to think that this Mr Marshall was *her* Mr Marshall from Friday night. Marshall wasn't such an unusual name. On top of that, *her* Mr Marshall was an accountant. What would an accountant be doing running an advertising agency, even temporarily?

'My name's Margaret, by the way,' the receptionist went on breezily. 'We might as well get to know each other. I probably shouldn't be saying this but I think you're more Mr Marshall's cup of tea than the girl who's in there now.'

'Why's that?' Jessie asked.

Somewhere on the floor a door banged.

'Judge for yourself,' Margaret murmured.

Just then this amazing creature swept down a corridor into the reception area.

The first thing that struck Jessie was her bright orange hair, which looked as if it had been cut with a chainsaw. A *rusty* chainsaw.

The second was the myriad gold studs and rings that adorned her starkly white face. Ears. Nose. Lips. Eyebrows. Chin.

Lord knew what other parts of her body had been pierced. Possibly a great many.

Thankfully, the girl was clothed from head to foot so Jessie could only speculate. Her style, however, was a combination of grunge and gothic and the garments she sported looked as if they'd been rescued from a charity bin. The kind they used for recycled rags.

'Tell Harry Wilde to contact me when he gets back, if he's still interested,' the escapee from the Addams Family tossed over her shoulder as she marched across the floor in her ex-army boots. 'I wouldn't work for him down there if he was the last man on earth. He knows absolutely nothing about the creative soul. Nothing!'

The moment she was gone Margaret looked over at a wide-eyed Jessie and grinned.

'See what I mean? I think you're a shoo-in.'

Jessie could not believe that fate had been so kind to her. 'I sure hope so. I really want this job.' She simply couldn't go the rest of her life being a waitress.

The reception phone buzzed and Margaret picked it up. 'Yes, Karen, I'll send her down straight away. And don't worry, he'll like *this* one. Your turn,' she said with an encouraging smile to Jessie as she hung up. 'Down to the end of that corridor. Go straight in.'

Jessie gulped, then stood up. 'Er—just one thing before I go. Do you happen to know Mr Marshall's first name?'

'Sure. It's Kane. Why?'

Jessie could not believe how relieved she felt. For a moment there…

She shrugged. 'I knew a guy named Marshall once and I was a bit worried this might be the same man. Thankfully, it isn't,' she muttered, and Margaret laughed.

'We all have one of those somewhere in our past.'

True. But the trouble was this one wasn't far enough in Jessie's past. He was only a couple of nights ago, and could still make her tremble at the thought of him.

Her nerves eased a lot with the surety that the Mr

Marshall about to interview her wasn't Curtis Marshall, married man and sexily irresistible hunk. She also couldn't deny she felt good that her competition had turned out so poorly. Clearly, Nicholas from Adstaff hadn't given carrot-top the same conservative-dressing advice he'd given her. Or if he had, she'd ignored him.

The door at the end of the corridor led into the PA's office. It wasn't quite as colourful as Reception, but still very nice and spacious and modern. Karen herself was nothing like Jessie had expected Harry Wilde's PA to be. She was forty-ish. A redhead. Pleasantly plump. And sweet.

'Oh, thank you, God!' she exclaimed on seeing Jessie. 'Did you see the other one?'

'Yes. Um. I did,' Jessie admitted. 'But to be honest, people like that are not unusual in the advertising world. She probably sees herself as an artiste with a certain avant-garde image to uphold.'

'We don't hire avant-garde artistes here,' Karen said wryly. 'We hire people with lots of innovative ideas who know how to work. And work hard. Now, did Margaret happen to mention that Mr Wilde's away right now?'

'Yes, she did.'

'Good. Then you'll understand why I'm doing part of your interview. Mr Marshall is an excellent manager and motivator, but he has no background in advertising. I've been with Mr Wilde a good few years and I know what he likes in an employee. I've already had a good look at your résumé, and I was impressed. Now that I can see you in person, I'm even more impressed. If you could just show me your portfolio, please?'

Jessie pulled out her portfolio and handed it over. She'd included samples of the best work she'd done over the years, plus mock-ups of ads she would like to do, if ever given the chance.

'Mmm. This is excellent. Michele is going to be pleased with you. Michele will be your boss. She's one of our top executives. Her assistant quit last week after they had an altercation over his lack of motivation. He's been having a lot of time off. A drug problem, we think. Anyway, she needs a good graphic artist to step into his shoes straight away. She has several things that need to be finished before the Christmas break. On top of that, she'll be going off on maternity leave in the middle of next year. She's having another baby. When that happens, we're hoping you'll be able to fill in for her. I gather from Adstaff that you do have ambitions to become a creative designer yourself, is that right?'

'It's my dearest wish. The sample ads at the back of my portfolio are my own original ideas. They're not actual campaigns I worked on.'

'Really. I hadn't quite got that far.' She flipped over some more pages of the portfolio, stopping to stare hard at one of the pages. 'Is this one of yours? This white-goods magazine ad,' Karen said, holding up a page.

'Yes, that's one I made up myself.'

The page had a vibrant blue background to highlight the white goods. In the middle was a dishwasher, washing machine and dryer, surrounded by other smaller kitchen appliances, all in stainless steel. Draped across the three taller items was a very glamorous Mae-West style blonde, her evening gown white with a very low neckline, her scarlet-tipped fingers caressing the appliances. Above her were the words, 'It's not the appliances in your life but the life in your appliances,' a parody of Mae West's famous comment, 'It's not the men in your life but the life in your men.'

'It's brilliant!' Karen exclaimed.

Jessie puffed up with pride. 'Thank you.'

'We have a new account for a kitchen-appliance company which this would be perfect for. I must show it to Peter. He's handling that account. I can see Michele and Peter fighting over you. Of course, Mr Marshall will have to hire you first,' she added with a grin. 'But I'm sure that's just a formality. Come on, let's get you in there. Hopefully, he's recovered from the last applicant by now. You should have seen his face when she walked in. My fault, of course. I was the one who picked her. Her résumé was impressive, but in reality she was not suitable at all.'

'Do you mind if I ask why not? Looks can be deceiving. She might have been very talented.'

'She was. A *very* talented graphic artist. But not suitable for promotion. Harry likes his front people to have a certain look, and style. After all, they have to deal with a wide range of clients, some of whom are very conservative. Harry believes first impressions are very important. Kane agrees with him. And you, Jessie Denton, make a very good first impression.'

'But I'm only wearing jeans.'

'Yes, but they're clean and neat, and you wear them with panache. And I simply love what you've done with your hair. Very classy.'

Jessie could not have felt more confident as she was ushered into Harry Wilde's office. Her self-esteem was sky-high, her heart beating with pleasurable anticipation, not nervous tension.

Fate had been good to her, for once.

But then the man seated behind Harry Wilde's desk looked up, and Jessie's heart literally stopped.

Oh, *no*, she groaned. How could this be? The receptionist had said his name was Kane, not Curtis!

But it *was* him. No doubt about it. She wasn't about to forget what he looked like, especially when he was even dressed the same, in a suit, shirt and tie.

His ice-blue eyes locked onto hers, his dark brows lifting in surprise. Or was it shock?

'Yes, I know what you mean,' Karen said to him with a small laugh. 'A definite improvement on Ms Jaegers. This is Jessie Denton. Here's her portfolio.' She walked forward and placed the folder on the wide walnut desk. 'I've had a good look at it and it's simply fabulous. Now, can I get either of you some coffee? Or tea?'

'No, thanks,' Jessie croaked out.

'Not at the moment, Karen,' her boss said.

'OK, I'll leave you to it.'

'Re*lax*,' she mouthed to a shell-shocked Jessie as she walked past her.

And then she was gone, shutting the door behind her.

Jessie just stood there in the middle of the large,
plushly furnished office, her shock slowly draining
away, anxiety rushing back. Anxiety and dismay.

Fate hadn't been kind to her at all. It had dangled
the most wonderful opportunity in front of her nose
like a carrot, only to snatch it away at the last moment. Because *this* Mr Marshall—regardless of what
his first name turned out to be—wasn't about to hire
her, no matter what she did, or said.

There was no way out.

If she told him the truth about why she'd been at
that bar last Friday night, he would feel both humil-
iated and threatened. If she didn't tell him the truth,
then she had to fall back on that other even more
sordid reality. That she'd fancied him like mad and
been tempted by him, despite knowing he was married.

No, that wasn't right, she suddenly realised. If she
kept her decoy work a secret, then she would not
have *known* he was married. He didn't wear a wed-
ding ring. She'd noticed that the other night.

In that case, how could she explain her sudden
disappearing act?

Saying simply that she'd changed her mind
seemed rather lame. She would come across as a
tease. She supposed she could say someone in the
ladies' room had warned her he was a married man
and that was why she'd done a flit.

That might salvage *her* pride and reputation, but
it wouldn't do much for his.

The main problem here was that *he'd* known he was a married man all along, and he'd still asked her to go to a hotel room with him.

Recalling that highly charged moment brought back to Jessie the feelings she had shared with him that night. The mutual attraction. The rush of desire. The heat.

She stared at him as a new wave of heat flowed through her body, flooding her from her toes right up into her face.

There *was* no way out of this, except out the door.

'I guess I might as well leave right now,' she choked out. 'Just give me my portfolio back, please, and I'll get going.'

CHAPTER SIX

KANE rarely felt panic, but he felt it now. She was running out on him. *Again!*

He couldn't let that happen. Not now that he'd found her. The thought that he would never see her again had haunted him all weekend.

Of course, it would help to know why she'd run out on him in the first place. The only reason he could imagine was that he must have come on too hard and too fast for her.

Now he didn't know what to think.

All he knew was that nothing had changed for him since Friday night. One look from those incredible eyes of hers and he'd been right back there on that dance floor, his body consumed by the need to sweep her off into bed.

Bed? He almost laughed at that notion. A bed would not do. This all-consuming passion he was suffering from demanded a much faster, harder surface to pin her to. A wall. A floor. This desk, even.

Kane swallowed. He was really losing it!

And he'd lose her again, if she knew what was going on his head.

'Last Friday night has no relevance whatsoever to today,' he said with astonishing composure. Lust was a very powerful motivation. 'That was pleasure. This is business. But perhaps we should get the past out of the way first. Would you care to sit down and tell me why you left the way you did?'

She frowned, but stayed standing. He tried to stop his eyes from continually raking her from head to toe, but truly she was a magnificent-looking woman. And so sexy in those tight jeans, it was criminal.

'What's the point?' she said sharply, brown eyes flashing. 'I can't work for you. You must know that.'

He didn't, actually. Was she worried about sexual harassment in the workplace?

Perhaps she had just cause, given how much he craved her right now. But Kane could exercise control and patience when necessary. *And* when she wasn't touching him. The last thing he wanted to do was frighten her off. She was the first woman in a long time who had made him feel what he'd felt on Friday night. To be honest, he couldn't recall *ever* feeling quite what he'd felt on that dance floor.

Usually, he could stay in control. Usually, his brain was always there in the background, analysing the situation, making judgement calls, warning him when the momentary object of his desire was another waste of his time.

But it hadn't on that occasion.

Maybe that was why she'd obsessed about him all weekend. The way she'd made him forget everything but the moment. He hadn't known anything at all about her, except that she went into sleazy bars alone, dressed to thrill. Not a great recommendation.

Yet he'd still wanted her like crazy.

He still did.

No way was he going to let her escape from him

a second time. He wanted to experience the magic he'd felt in her arms once more. Too bad if it didn't go anywhere. He was sick and tired of thinking about the future and working his life to a plan. He'd got into a rather boring rut over the years. He'd forgotten how to be impulsive.

He wanted this woman, and he was going to have her, whether she was good for him or not.

'But you won't really be working for *me*,' he replied smoothly. 'You'll be working for Harry Wilde. I'm just the caretaker manager till Christmas, which is less than two weeks away now. After that, any boss-employee relationship between us is over.'

She still stared at him with wary eyes and he wondered why. Damn it all, she fancied him. He knew she did. She'd been with him all the way on Friday night, till she'd gone to the ladies'.

He'd been stunned when she hadn't showed up again.

'So what *did* happen on Friday night?' he asked, his teeth clenched firmly in his jaw. 'Did you just change your mind? Was that it?'

'I...I...'

Her fluster was telling. And quite enchanting. Maybe she wasn't the tease he'd been thinking she might be. Or a serial good-time girl, the kind who cruised bars at night looking for some cheap fun and excitement.

'It's not a crime to change your mind, Jessie,' he said gently. Though it had felt like it at the time. He'd been furious.

'I didn't change my mind,' she said, which totally confused him.

'What, then?'

Jessie felt she had to come up with some explanation, or look a right fool.

'A girl in the ladies' told me you were married,' she blurted out. 'I...I don't sleep with married men.'

There was no doubt her excuse startled him. His head jerked back and he blinked a couple of times. But then he did the strangest thing.

He smiled.

'Married,' he said with a low chuckle. 'How come I didn't think of that? *Married!*' And he laughed again.

'I don't think it's funny,' she snapped. She knew a lot of modern people didn't take marital vows seriously. But she did.

'Aah, but it is funny. Because I'm *not* married,' came his astonishing announcement. 'My brother is, however. My twin brother. My *identical* twin brother. He's been frequenting that particular bar every Friday night for a while, so it's understandable that someone made a mistake, thinking I was him.'

Jessie opened her mouth, then closed it again. The man she'd flirted with, and wanted so badly on Friday night, hadn't been her target at all. It had been this man, Kane Marshall, Curtis Marshall's twin brother!

As amazing as this revelation was, it did explain the small differences between the target's photograph and the man in front of her. His hairstyle. The colour of his eyes. And his whole personality. The man in the photograph had seemed softer.

There was nothing soft about Kane Marshall.

A second realisation hit Jessie with even more force. Kane Marshall was single. And available. There was absolutely no reason why she couldn't say yes if he ever asked her out.

Which he would. She could see it in his eyes.

A thrill—or was it a chill?—rippled down her spine. So much for her decision not to have a man in her life.

Of course, she hadn't anticipated at the time that she could possibly have *this* man. He was a whole different ballgame.

'You're *definitely* not married?' she asked.

'Definitely not. My divorce came through a few months ago.'

This added news didn't thrill her. She wasn't sure why. Perhaps because most of the recently divorced guys she'd met were always on the make. It was as though after casting aside their wives, sex was the *only* thing on their minds. They were always on the hunt for new prey. She'd met quite a few newly divorced men at the restaurant and they usually gave her the creeps, the way they looked at her, and the way they assumed she'd be easy meat.

Was that what Kane Marshall had thought of her on Friday night, that she was easy meat? She'd gone into that bar alone, after all. Why would a girl go into a bar alone on a Friday night, if not to pick up some guy? The only excuse she'd given him for not going to a hotel room with him was that someone had told her he was married.

Now that he knew she knew he wasn't, he had to be assuming she'd fall into bed with him next time without a qualm.

As much as the *idea* of falling into bed with him was incredibly exciting, Jessie knew that the reality might not be wise.

'No wife,' he stated firmly. 'No children. And no current girlfriend. Just so we don't have any more misunderstandings.'

Jessie blinked. That was sure laying his cards on the table. Next thing he'd be telling her if he had any communicable diseases!

'So are you quite happy to work here now?' he went on.

'Are you offering me the job?'

'Absolutely.'

'But you haven't even looked at my portfolio!'

'No need. I trust Karen's judgement regarding your creative talents. She has much more experience in this field than I do. I just wanted to see you in the flesh, to make sure you had the presence and style that Harry requires in his executives.'

Jessie frowned over his words, 'in the flesh'. Maybe his offering her this job had nothing to do with her talents and everything to do with his wanting to see *more* of her in the flesh, so to speak.

Still, if she was strictly honest with herself, she wanted the same thing. Whenever his eyes were upon her—which was all the time—she could think of nothing but being in his arms once more.

Hadn't she come to the conclusion at one stage over the weekend that she needed a man in her life? A boyfriend? A lover? Why not Kane Marshall? He wasn't married. Clearly, he fancied her as much as she fancied him. Crazy to fight an attraction as strong as this was. She would only lose.

'Even if I wasn't comparing you to the last applicant,' he went on suavely, 'I would be suitably impressed, and very happy to offer you the job. If *you're* still interested, that is.'

Jessie suspected he was asking her if she was still interested in him, as well as the job.

'Yes, of course I am,' she said, deciding it would be hypocritical to say anything else.

'Good,' he said, then delivered another of those dazzling smiles of his.

He was smooth! And incredibly confident.

He both excited and rattled her. A strange combination. She'd always been attracted to physically strong men, but Kane Marshall represented more than just physical strength. His persona carried exceptional charisma. A magnetism which perturbed her. His steely gaze had the capacity to sap her willpower. But it was his sexy smile that could do the most damage. She suspected that if they became lovers, he could make her *do* things. Wild things. Wicked things.

Her thoughts sent an erotically charged quiver rippling down her spine. Suddenly, her knees felt like jelly.

'I...I think I'd better sit down,' she said, reefing her eyes away from his and pulling up one of the upright wooden chairs adjacent to the desk. She sank down onto its solid surface, grateful not to have to look at him for a while. But eventually, she had to face him once more. When she did, her shoulders were rammed back against the chair-back, her back was as stiff as a board and her legs were tightly crossed.

Her rigid body language was wasted, however. He wasn't looking at her. His handsome face was down, and he was going through what looked like her résumé.

'I see here that you're a single mother,' he remarked before finally glancing back up at her.

Jessie's chin lifted defiantly. 'Is that a problem?'

'Absolutely not. I admire unmarried women who keep their babies,' he added with warmth in his voice and another of those winning smiles.

'I meant, is that a problem with my job?' she bit out, irritated with herself for going to mush inside again.

'I don't see why it should be. You have your little girl in day-care, it says here.'

'Yes, but there will be times when she gets sick. Or I might have to attend a school concert. Or some emergency.'

'Work conditions here at Wild Ideas are very flexible. You can work your own hours, or at home if you want. All that is required is that the work is done, meetings are attended and deadlines met. Your immediate boss is the mother of a little girl herself, with another baby on the way, so I'm sure she will be very understanding about such matters. Speaking of Michele, I think perhaps I should take you along to meet her shortly. She rang earlier with instructions to have someone sitting at the computer by her side before lunchtime. Or else.'

'You mean you want me to start straight away, *today*?' Jessie gasped.

He raised a single eyebrow at her. 'I thought you understood that. Is there any reason you *have* to leave?'

'No…no, I guess not. But I will have to ring the day-care centre and tell them I'll be a bit later than usual picking Emily up.'

'Will that worry your little girl?'

'No. But it might worry me. I'm not sure how often the trains run and how long it will take me to get there. I have to pick Emily up before six. They close at six.'

'You don't have a car?'

'No,' she admitted. 'I haven't been able to afford to run one.'

'You should be able to now. Your pay is sixty-five thousand dollars a year, with bonuses.'

All the breath was punched from Jessie's lungs. 'You're joking! Sixty-five thousand?' Before she'd had Emily, she'd only been on forty thousand.

'That's right. Your basic salary will be reviewed every six months, with rises given on performance.'

'That's incredible.'

'Don't worry. You'll have to deliver.'

'I'll deliver. Don't you worry about that.'

Their eyes met once more, with Jessie wondering if their conversation still carried a double meaning.

She hoped not. She'd hate to think that underneath his impressive surface, Kane Marshall was just another divorced creep.

'You should consider leasing a car,' he went on. 'Curtis always tells me that leasing is a much more sensible option in business. My brother is an accountant,' he added.

Unnecessarily. Jessie already knew that. But she could hardly say so. Still, it sent her wondering exactly where Kane Marshall usually worked. Karen had said he was an excellent manager and motivator. But for what company?

'If you like,' he was saying, 'I could get Karen to organise the leasing for you. All you have to do is tell me what kind of car you'd like.'

'I...I don't really know. I'll have to think about it.'

'If you tell me the make and model in the morning, it can be ready for you by the time you finish up tomorrow. Meanwhile, I'm quite happy to drive you home after work tonight. I wouldn't want you to worry about your little girl.'

Jessie stared at him. He certainly wasn't wasting any time in making his move.

'You don't have to do that,' she said. 'I do have a friend I could ring to pick Emily up if I think I can't make it.'

'A man friend?'

The question sounded casual, but Jessie could see more than curiosity in his eyes. Insane to imagine he was jealous. But it felt as if he was.

'No,' she said, and was sure he looked relieved.

'An elderly lady. My landlady, in fact. I rent a granny flat from her. But she's also a good friend.'

'It's no trouble for me to drive you home, Jessie,' he said. 'You don't live that far away. Besides, I'd like the opportunity to talk to you some more. Out of the office.'

'All right, then,' she agreed, if a bit stiffly. She wished she could get the thought out of her head that she was being weak. 'Thank you.'

'It's my pleasure.' And he smiled at her again.

Jessie suppressed a moan. Oh, he was just so gorgeous. How could she possibly say no?

Yet she hated for him to think she was easy.

Jessie was well used to the way most men thought about single mothers. They were considered desperates. Desperate for sex. Desperate for company. Desperate for some man—*any* man—to give them the emotional and financial support they obviously weren't getting from whoever had fathered their child.

In truth, there were quite a lot of single mothers who did act that way.

But Jessie wasn't normally like most single mothers. She'd always prided herself on her self-sufficiency. After Lyall, she'd never wanted to rely on any man for anything. Not even for sex.

Not till she'd met Kane Marshall.

Now he was all she could think about. Already, she was looking forward to his driving her home. Her skin actually broke into goose-pimples at the thought.

Yet she should have been concentrating on the job she'd just been given.

Jessie jumped to her feet. 'Now that that's all settled, I'd better get started, don't you think?'

He was much slower in rising, buttoning up his jacket as he did so.

His action drew her eyes to his suit. It wasn't the same pale grey number he'd worn on Friday night. This one was a darker grey. But it was just as expensive-looking and stylish. Not a wrinkle marred the line of its sleeves, or where the collar sat neatly around his solid neck.

He was a big man, she noticed once more. Not overweight. Just tall, and strong, with the broadest shoulders.

He would look good, naked. *Feel* good, too.

Oh, dear, Jessie groaned to herself. I'm in trouble here. Big, big trouble.

'This way,' he said as he walked around and gestured towards the door.

Thankfully he didn't touch her. His eyes were bad enough. The way they kept running over her.

He wasn't all that different from those other divorced creeps who'd pursued her, Jessie realised as she bolted through the door ahead of him.

The difference lay in her. Those other men hadn't made her tremble with a look. They hadn't made her forget every wise word of warning her mother had ever given her about men.

No, that wasn't true. She hadn't forgotten any of her mother's warnings. She knew what Kane Marshall was, and what he wanted.

The difference this time was that she wanted exactly the same thing he did.

CHAPTER SEVEN

JESSIE could not believe how quickly the day went, and how nice everyone was at Wild Ideas, especially her immediate boss.

In her early thirties, Michele was an attractive brunette, married, with one little girl and another baby on the way. She was warm and welcoming to Jessie, but at the same time efficient and precise. *Very* precise with her directions. She knew what she wanted—art-wise—and expected things to be done exactly as she wanted.

But Jessie was used to that. Jackson & Phelps had been a demanding company to work for. They had high standards and had trained her well.

But she much preferred working for Wild Ideas. Such a friendly atmosphere. The staff was relatively small—about twenty—and pretty well everyone had popped their heads into Michele's office at some time during the day.

Actually, calling it an office was misleading. It was more of a work station. The behind-the-scenes office layout at Wild Ideas was open plan, cut up into cubicles, some larger than others. Michele's area was quite large, but not fancy in any way. Plain pine furniture. No carpet. No doors. One window that looked out on to the main road.

Still, everything in it was clean and functional,

with state-of-the-art computer equipment, along with every piece of software imaginable. Jessie got very excited to work on the very latest G5 Macintosh, which was so much faster than her old Imac.

Just as well, because her predecessor had left things in a right mess. There was so much to sort through that when lunchtime came she ate a sandwich at her desk. Margaret from Reception dropped by and brought her some coffee, which was sweet of her. Jessie could see that they were going to become friends.

The only breaks she had were to go to the ladies' room and to make three phone calls. The first was to the restaurant to say that she was quitting. Since she was only a casual anyway, they didn't much care. They'd fill her spot within hours. The second was to the day-care centre. True to form, Emily didn't give a hoot that she would be late picking her up. Traitorous child! The third was to Dora, who was thrilled Jessie had got the job.

Unfortunately, Jessie couldn't explain about the fiasco with the Marshall brothers, not with Michele sitting right next to her.

Actually, Jessie liked it that she worked right beside Michele and wasn't off in another section on the floor, either in a corner by herself or with a whole bunch of other graphic artists. It seemed that at Wild Ideas, each creative designer had their own personal graphic artist. Sort of like their own private assistant. Jessie could see that this was a very successful way of doing things. New team leaders were being trained all the time. No wonder Harry Wilde never had to head-hunt executives from other agencies. He didn't need to.

'Time to wrap it up for today, girls. It's almost five.'

Jessie whipped her head round at Kane's voice to find him leaning against the open door frame, watching her. He looked as if he'd been there a while.

Actually, she'd surprised herself, the way she'd been able to put the man out of her mind for most of the day. But the moment their eyes met once more, all the feelings he evoked in her rushed back.

Not just heart-pounding desire. That was a given. But accompanying jabs of panic, and worry.

Her life since Emily had been born had been so simple. And straightforward. Maybe a little boring. And yes, lonely at times. But not too stressful.

If she became involved with Kane Marshall—even on just a casual basis—he would begin to make demands on her time and her space. As a single mother who now had a full-time job, Jessie knew she wouldn't have much spare time for leisure and pleasure.

'So how did our new girl work out, Michele?' Kane asked.

'Excellent,' Michele replied crisply. 'She's very good at what she does. And I suspect she'll be very good at what I do. Eventually,' she added with a cheeky wink.

Jessie didn't know what to say in reply to such fulsome praise, so she said nothing.

'We'd better get going, Jessie,' Kane asked. 'The traffic will be heavy. I'm driving Jessie home today,' he explained to Michele. 'She has to pick her daughter up by six and she's not sure about the train timetable.'

'Yes, I know. Jessie told me all about your knight-to-the-rescue act,' Michele said drily, a slightly knowing smile playing on her mouth. 'Off you go, love. And thanks for all your hard work. See you tomorrow at eight-thirty.'

'Eight-thirty?' Kane echoed. 'I thought the hours here were nine to five.'

'Jessie and I had a talk and we decided eight-thirty till four-thirty would suit us better. We're both up early with our children anyway. Might as well get them to day-care and get to work. Then we'll have more time to spend with them in the evening.'

'Whatever.' Kane shrugged his broad shoulders, his nonchalance reminding Jessie that men like Kane didn't have to worry about making time for children. All they had to think about was themselves.

Men did that very well, she reminded herself. So don't go thinking he's driving you home because he's genuinely kind. He's driving you home because he wants to get into your pants.

Jessie was appalled when this thought didn't repulse her, as it normally would. Maybe she shouldn't have stayed celibate this long. Suppressing a sigh, she turned off her computer, picked up her bag and stood up.

'Bye, Michele. Thanks for being so nice. See you in the morning.'

'She *is* a nice woman, isn't she?' Kane said as they

rode the lift down to the basement car park. He
sounded surprised.

'Very,' Jessie agreed. 'Good at her job, too,' she
added, determined not to let her secret thoughts and
desires make her go all stiff and awkward with him
again.

'Harry doesn't hire any other kind,' Kane com-
mented.

'I hope he won't be disappointed with me when
he gets back.'

'I'm sure he won't be, Jessie. This way,' he directed when the lift doors opened.

She was glad when he didn't get all handy once
they were alone in the car park. She wasn't keen on
guys who used any opportunity to grab at a girl.

'Here we are,' he said, stopping beside a sleek
silver sedan. Inside, she noticed, it had grey leather
seats and that lovely new smell. Jessie didn't know
what the make was and she didn't ask. She knew
next to nothing about cars. Which reminded her...

'By the way, I won't be leasing a car just yet,' she
advised him as he drove expertly round the circular
ramp that led to the street.

'Why not?'

'I don't like to rush into things. I like to think
about them first before taking the plunge.'

'Is that a learned habit, a statement of fact, or a
warning for me?'

'Do you need a warning?'

The car emerged into the late-afternoon sunshine,
and very heavy traffic. Kane's very masculine mouth

remained shut till they stopped at the first set of lights.

'Jessie, let's not play games with each other,' he said firmly. 'You came into that bar the other night looking for male company. If you hadn't been told I was a married man, we'd already be lovers.'

Jessie decided then and there that the time had come for the truth. Her pride demanded she not let him think she made a habit of cruising bars at night, picking up perfect strangers and agreeing to go to hotel rooms with them.

'No one in the ladies' told me you were a married man, Kane,' she confessed, her chin lifting as she turned her head his way. 'I made that up.'

'You *what*? But why? I mean... Oh, go to hell!' he muttered into the rear-vision mirror. The lights had gone green and the driver behind was honking his horn.

'Look, just drive and listen!' she told him in that tone she used on Emily when she wouldn't go to bed at night.

Once he got over his shock at her giving him orders like that, he actually obeyed. The silence gave her the opportunity to tell him the truth, starting with her working as a decoy earlier this year when she hadn't had any money. She explained how she hated it and had quit, but agreed to do it one last time so that she could buy Emily the expensive fairy doll for Christmas.

He *did* throw her a startled look when she said she'd only gone into that bar last Friday night to do a decoy job. When she revealed who her target was, his car almost careered into the wrong lane. She had to tell him to keep his eyes on the road again, after which she was able to finish her story. She even mentioned that she hadn't labelled his brother a potentially unfaithful husband because Kane had knocked back the blonde.

'Of course, I didn't know at the time,' she added, 'that it was *you* knocking back the blonde and not your brother, Curtis.'

Kane was speechless at first. Then a bit stroppy.

'Well, thank you very much for not ruining my brother's marriage! Why didn't you? Guilt?'

'*Guilt?* Why should I feel guilty?'

'Come on, doll, let's face it. If I had been some poor, unhappily married bloke, and you'd swanned into that bar making eyes at me whilst I was sloshed, I'd have had a hard job resisting you, too.'

'Don't exaggerate,' she said. 'I'm not that sexy.'

'Trust me, sweetheart, you are. You're one hell of an actress, too. I could have sworn you were genuinely turned on last Friday night, that you really wanted me to make love to you.'

This was her out, if she wanted to take it.

Jessie decided on a middle course.

'I *did* find you rather attractive,' she admitted with considerable understatement. 'But I would never have gone to a hotel room with you. Not within minutes of meeting you.'

That was her story and she was going to stick to it.

'I didn't know your name, either,' he muttered. 'But I couldn't have given a damn.'

'Yes, well, you're a man. You're a different spe-
cies entirely. Women are, on the whole, a little more
careful.'

'Not all women,' he ground out.

Possibly, he was remembering the blonde.

'I do realise that. I also realise that single mothers
have a certain reputation for being…shall we
say…easy marks? I wouldn't like you to make that
mistake if you're thinking of asking me out. Which
I presume you are. Because why else would you be
here, driving me home?'

Another set of lights brought the car to a halt. His
head turned till his eyes met hers once more. He
smiled wryly.

'You seem to have me taped perfectly. What can
I say? Yes, I want to ask you out. And yes, up till
now, my intentions have not been entirely honourable.'

'And now?'

'I still want to take you to bed. But I also want to
spend time with you out of bed. You're a very intriguing woman, Jessie Denton.'

Jessie felt herself blushing. She turned her head
away to stare out at the halted traffic, which was
thicker than when they'd left north Sydney. She
glanced at her watch. It was almost half-past five and
they were only at Chatswood. Still, once they got
through this bottleneck it should be plainer sailing to
Roseville. They should arrive before six. But it
would be much quicker on the train.

'So will you go out with me?' he persisted.

Jessie turned back to face the road ahead. She

could feel him looking at her but refused to look his way again. Those eyes of his made her melt almost as much as his smile.

'Maybe,' she said, pleased with her cool tone.

'When?'

'Don't rush me, Kane.'

Kane. She'd called him Kane. She couldn't remember calling him that before.

'How about this Friday night?' he jumped in immediately. 'You must have had someone mind your daughter last Friday night. You could do the same this Friday night. We could go out to dinner, then on to a club, or whatever you like to do. The movies. A show. Anything.'

Going to bed with him would be nice, she thought, shocking herself again. Truly, she was in a bad way. But her pride was still greater than her need.

'I'm not sure about this Friday,' she said. 'I still don't know all that much about you. I mean, you've at least read my résumé. I don't even know what you usually do for a living, when you're not minding the store for Harry Wilde.'

'You'll find the answer to that question on your desk in the morning. Easier than trying to explain what I do. It would take all night.'

Jessie blinked over at him. He called her intriguing. He was the intriguing one.

'OK, but I still don't know much about you personally. I mean, you said you were divorced. How long were you married and why did your wife divorce you?'

'We were married for three years and *I* was the one who asked for a divorce.'

'Good heavens. Why? Was she unfaithful?' The idea seemed ludicrous to Jessie. If Kane were her husband she would never look at another man.

'Not that I know of.' The lights went green and the car crawled on through the busy intersection. 'My wife and I had a difference of opinion about the matter of having children,' he explained. 'We should have discussed it before we got married, I suppose, but… Did you see that bloke cut me off?'

She did and it was a near miss. Still, they weren't going fast enough to have a serious prang.

'Driving a four-wheel-drive, of course,' Kane ground out angrily. 'Worse than truck drivers, they are. Why any sane person would need a mini-tank to get around the city I have no idea. They should all be banned. Now, where was I? Oh, yes, my divorce. Look, when I realised that I couldn't change my wife's mind about having kids, I decided to call it quits. It was quite an amicable parting. We're still very good friends.'

Jessie couldn't help feeling disappointed that Kane was one of those selfish modern men who didn't want children. Truly, he should never have got married in the first place. That poor woman, wasting three years of her life on a man who would never give her what she wanted.

Which was a good warning for herself.

'I see,' she said, nodding.

'And what about you, Jessie?' he counter-questioned whilst she was still pondering if it was worth the risk of falling in love with Kane Marshall, just to have the pleasure of going to bed with him.

'Why aren't you still with the father of your child?'

She could have told him the long version. But she decided he probably wouldn't be interested.

'He died,' she said. 'In a snowboarding accident. Before Emily was born.'

'God, how awful!' He seemed genuinely shocked and sympathetic. 'That's tragic, Jessie. Truly, I'm very sorry. I hope his family has been supportive.'

'I never told them about the baby. Lyall was estranged from his folks, and frankly, I didn't like the sound of them. Anyway, they live over in New Zealand. I could hardly afford to fly over all the time. I thought it best to raise Emily by myself.'

'But what about your own folks?'

Jessie winced. 'Not a pretty picture there either, I'm afraid. Mum was a single mother herself. My father was a married man. She was Irish and Catholic, so getting rid of me was out of the question. Anyway, she emigrated to Australia when I was a baby, by which time she was all bitter and twisted about men. A few years ago she went back home. She wasn't at all pleased about my becoming a single mother. Said I was a fool. But I'm a very different single mother from my mum, I can tell you.'

'I don't doubt it. You're one very strong character, Jessie Denton. Very brave.'

'Brave?' Jessie gave that notion some thought. 'Not really. I was scared stiff at the time. Not to mention seriously depressed. I didn't have post-natal depression. I had pre-natal depression. But I couldn't have done anything else. Emily was my baby. And really, other than having a few money worries, it's been an incredible experience. I wouldn't change a day of it. And now that I've got a decent job, I won't even have any money worries,' she added, not wanting him to think she needed money from any man. Or that she might look at him as a possible meal ticket.

'I read on your résumé that you've been working as a waitress,' he said. 'Did you like doing that?'

Jessie shrugged. 'Not overly. But it was the only job I could get other than decoy work. And I couldn't bear doing that on a regular basis. I only did it this one last time for the money. Do you have any idea how much a Felicity Fairy doll costs?'

'Actually, yes, I do. I've been instructed to buy one for my niece for Christmas. She's about the same age as your Emily. Maybe we could go Christmas shopping together.'

She slanted him a wry smile. 'You planning on seducing me amongst the soft-toy section of Sydney's biggest department store? Save yourself the price of a dinner?'

He laughed. 'I can't see any man seducing you on the cheap, Jessie.'

'One did. *Once,*' she added tartly. 'And I ended up with Emily.'

'So I'm being punished for some other man's mis-deeds, am I?'

'Let's just say I look before I leap these days. But you're out of luck. Dora bought Emily's doll for me last Saturday. So you'll have to go Felicity Fairy shopping by yourself. A word of advice, however. Do it soon or there won't be any left to buy.'

'I'll do that. We're getting close to Roseville. I might need some directions soon.'

Jessie glanced at her watch again. 'We'll only just make it in time.'

'What happens if you're late?'

'There are penalty rates for every quarter of an hour you keep them waiting after six o'clock.'

'That's rough. What if there was an accident and the traffic was backed up for miles?'

'Indeed,' she said drily. 'That's why I'll be catching the train in future. But it gives you a little inkling of the stresses and strains of being a working mother. Not much time left over for extra-curricular activities, either. Take the next corner on the left. The day-care centre is four blocks down, on the left. It's cement-rendered, painted pale blue. You can't miss it.'

'Would you go to work if you didn't have to?' he asked as he swung round the corner.

'I don't *have* to work. I could stay at home on welfare. But I don't think that's much of an example to Emily as she grows up. I think if you can work, you should. On top of that, it's nice to have some extra money. Welfare sucks, I can tell you.'

'What if you were married, and your husband earned a good income? Would you work then?'

Jessie laughed. 'I don't indulge in futile fantasies, Kane.'

'I was thinking of my brother's wife, Lisa. She's been a stay-at-home mum for over four years. I thought she was happy but she's not. I advised her this weekend to get a baby-sitter in a bit more often and join a gym. But I have a feeling that's just a temporary solution. I think she needs more.'

'She should find a good day-care centre and go back to work, even if it's only part-time. Or do some voluntary work, if she doesn't need the money. She needs adult company occasionally. And challenges outside of motherhood and wifery.'

'Yes,' Kane said. 'That's good advice. Thanks, Jessie. You might just have saved my brother's marriage for a second time. Aah, there's the place. And it's still only two minutes to six. We've made it!'

'Only just,' Jessie said, scrambling out of the car as soon as Kane slid into the kerb. 'Thanks a lot, Kane. Please don't wait. You've been very kind but you can go home now. It's only a ten-minute walk for me and Emily from here. We'll be fine. Bye. See you tomorrow.'

She didn't wait for him to argue with her, just slammed the passenger door and dashed inside.

Kane stared after her, then broke into a wry grin.

'You don't get rid of me as easy as that, honey,' he muttered.

Switching off the car engine, he climbed out from behind the wheel and walked around to the pavement, where he leant against the passenger door, folded his arms and waited patiently for Jessie to return.

CHAPTER EIGHT

SHE emerged after only two minutes, leading a little clone of herself by the hand. Black curly hair. Pale skin. Square jaw.

Jessie's expression, when she saw him waiting for her by his car, was a mixture of surprise and irritation. Her daughter's big brown eyes carried curiosity and delight.

Introductions were made rather reluctantly, with Jessie calling him Mr Marshall.

Emily gave him an odd look. Some of the delight had gone out of her eyes. 'Are you my mummy's new boss?' she asked. 'The one who made her late?'

'I am,' Kane confessed. 'But I'm going to make it up to you both by driving you home, then ordering a couple of pizzas to eat for dinner so that Mummy doesn't have to cook tonight.'

He'd opened both passenger doors invitingly whilst delivering this plan for the evening to a frowning Emily. When he glanced up at Jessie to find out her reaction, a rather strange smile was playing on her generous mouth.

'Is there a problem with that idea?' he asked, looking from mother to daughter.

'Mummy won't let me go in any car that hasn't got a proper car seat,' Emily announced primly whilst Mummy just kept on smiling. 'And Mummy won't let me eat pizzas. She says they're rubbish.'

'Aah. Headed off at the pass,' Kane muttered. 'Calls for right-flank action. OK, how about I walk home with you and Mummy? That way I'll know where you live for future reference. Then I can come back and get the car whilst you find out from your mummy what I *can* buy you both for dinner.'

'We always eat with Dora on a Monday,' the little powerhouse of information countered. 'Today is a Monday. Isn't that right, Mummy?'

'Yes, sweetie,' her mother said. With great satisfaction in her voice, Kane noted ruefully.

'Checkmate, I think,' Jessie added with a wicked gleam in her eyes.

Kane's teeth clenched hard in his jaw. He'd see those eyes glitter for a different reason one day. Or he wasn't the guy voted most likely to succeed!

'Is that the correct metaphor?' he asked, his soft voice belying his hard resolve. 'Besides, chess is just a game. This is war. I will reconsider my tactics on the way to your house.'

Slamming the car doors, he zapped the lock, slipped the keys in his trouser pocket, then faced the enemy with one of his how-to-win-friends-and-influence-people smiles.

'May I carry your bag for you, little lady?' he offered, reaching for the small backpack which Emily had been dragging along the pavement.

'I can carry my own bag, thank you very much,' she informed him pertly. Although she needed her mother's help to put it on.

Kane slanted Jessie a droll look. 'A new feminist in training?'

'No. An independent spirit. Everyone needs to be one of those these days to survive.'

'You could be right. OK, how about *you* carry the bag, Emily, but I'll carry *you*?'

Without waiting for her next objection, Kane hoicked Emily up to sit on his shoulders, one leg on each side of his head. She really was very light, even with a bag on her back.

'You wrap your arms around my neck and I'll hold your feet,' he told her. But when he grabbed her sandal-clad feet, a shower of sand sprayed down the front of his designer suit.

'What the…?'

'Emily spends a good deal of each afternoon in the sandpit,' Jessie explained without any apologies.

'Right,' Kane said through gritted teeth.

'It'll brush off easily enough,' Jessie told him blithely. 'Here… Look…'

He stiffened when she started brushing him down.

'I think the sand's all gone now,' he said curtly after a minute's torture.

She kept on doing it. 'I don't want you blaming me for ruining your lovely suit. Italian, is it?'

'Yes.' He named its designer.

She rolled her eyes at him. 'I should have guessed.'

At last, she took her hands off him.

'OK, you've been returned to your usual sartorial splendour. Let's walk.'

Kane was very relieved to walk. Still, his reaction

to her merely brushing his hands down over his chest gave him an inkling of how incredible it would be to have her touch him without clothes on.

'It's fun!' Emily's excited voice brought Kane back to the moment in hand. He'd loved riding on his father's shoulders as a child.

'It's a bit like horse-riding,' he said. 'Have you ever been horse-riding, Emily?'

'Yeah, I take her every weekend,' Jessie muttered under her breath beside him. 'When I can fit it in between the ballet and the violin lessons.'

Fortunately, Emily didn't hear her mother's sarcasm.

'No, I haven't,' she said politely. 'Mummy, can I go horse-riding?' she asked in all innocence.

'There aren't any horses in the city, sweetie,' Jessie replied. 'We'd have to drive out into the country and we'd need a car for that. We don't have a car.'

'I'll take you,' Kane said, and was rewarded with the most savage glare from Jessie.

'You don't have to do that,' she bit out.

'But I want to,' he said. 'I'd enjoy it.'

And it was true. He would enjoy it.

'When?' Emily chimed in. 'When?'

'Soon,' Kane promised.

'Not till after Christmas,' Jessie intervened abruptly. 'We're all too busy before Christmas. On top of that, Mr Marshall would have to get a proper child seat before we could go anywhere in his car. Such things take time.'

Her slightly smug smile suggested to Kane that she

thought that getting a car seat would be just too much trouble.

'Kane,' he said firmly. 'You are to call me Kane. *Not* Mr Marshall.'

'Very well. This way...*Kane*.'

She led him round a corner that brought them into a tree-lined street that was much quieter than the road the day-care centre was on. Emily had fun picking leaves off the trees, her happy chatter distracting the two adults from their verbal foreplay.

Because that was what it was. Kane knew it, even if Jessie didn't. She wanted him as much as he wanted her. She was just too cynical about men to give in to her desire and just go with the flow. She thought if she delayed the inevitable, Christmas would come, he'd leave Wild Ideas and that would be that. Out of the office and out of her life.

Kane refused to be deterred. The more difficult she was, the more he was determined to have her, not just in his bed, but in his life. His feelings might not be true love as yet, but they were more than lust. Oh, yes, much more.

Five minutes later, she stopped to open the front gate of a delightful old Federation house. It had a lovely rose garden on either side of a paved front path that led up to an enclosed front porch and a front door with stained-glass panels on either side.

Dear Dora, it seemed, was not exactly poor. Homes like this in Roseville were not cheap. Kane wondered if she rented out her granny flat to Jessie and Emily more for the company than the money.

'I'll have to put you down now, Emily,' he said

as he approached the front steps. 'Otherwise you'll hit your head on the porch roof.'

Jessie's heart turned over as she watched Kane lift Emily off his shoulders and set her gently down. The look of adoration that her child gave him made her want to hit the bastard.

Because that was what he was being. A right bastard. Using Emily to get to her.

Well, it wasn't going to work. She wasn't going to bed with him now, no matter how much she'd wanted to when she'd been brushing him down a few minutes back. The man was built, all right. Clearly, he worked out a lot.

Dora must have heard them arrive because she whisked open the front door before anyone rang the bell.

Jessie had to laugh at the look on her face when she saw Kane.

'This is Mr Marshall,' Emily piped up. 'Mummy's new boss. But he likes to be called Kane. He wanted to drive us home but he didn't have a car seat for me, so Mummy said no. But his car is lovely,' she rattled on. 'It's very shiny and silver. He's going to take me in it to go horse-riding after Christmas. He's going to have a car seat by then. He wanted to buy us pizza tonight but Mummy said no. Can he come to dinner, Dora? You always cook too much food. Mummy said so last Monday night.'

Jessie was besieged by a mixture of pride that her four-year-old daughter could talk so well, and embarrassment at the ingenuous content of her chatter.

Dora just laughed. She was used to Emily. Kane looked genuinely enchanted, which confused Jessie to no end. Was he that good an actor, or did he really like Emily?

She would have thought a man who didn't want his own children would be more impatient and less kind.

He must really want to go to bed with me an awful lot, Jessie decided, not sure if she felt flattered or infuriated.

'I'll have to pop a few extra potatoes in,' Dora said. 'It's roast lamb tonight. Do you like roast lamb, Mr Marshall?'

'Love it. And it's Kane, remember?'

'Kane,' Dora repeated. 'But I thought…' And she threw Jessie a frowning glance.

'Would you believe Kane has a twin brother named Curtis?' Jessie replied. 'An *identical* twin brother? He's married, whereas Kane is divorced.'

'Really?' Dora said, enlightenment in her eyes. 'Fancy that!'

'Yes,' Jessie agreed drily. 'Fancy that.'

'I haven't got any brothers or sisters,' Emily said with a sigh. 'That's because my daddy died.'

'Yes, your mummy told me about that, Emily,' Kane said, squatting down to her height. 'That was very sad. But you're sure to get a new daddy one day. Your mummy's a very pretty lady. Would you like a new daddy?'

Before Emily had a chance to reply, Jessie hurried over and swept her up into her arms. 'Enough idle chit-chat. We have to get Emily bathed and changed before dinner. Why don't you stay and talk with Dora, Kane, while I do that? Dora, ply our guest here with some of your cream sherry. That should keep him out of mischief.'

'I don't ever drink and drive,' Kane replied, an amused lift to the corner of his mouth. 'But I'm sure Dora and I can find plenty of subjects to talk about whilst I watch her cook.' And he gave Jessie a look which implied that by the time she returned for Dora's roast-lamb dinner, he'd know everything there was to know about her.

She and Dora had had many deep and meaningful discussions over the last year or so, and women, un-like men, usually told the truth about themselves. A clever questioner could find out anything he wanted to know.

Jessie suspected she'd just made a tactical error.

But it was too late now.

She comforted herself with the knowledge that no matter what Kane discovered, she still had her own mind, and her own will-power. He couldn't force her to do anything she didn't want to do.

The trouble was that deep down, in that hidden woman's place which she'd been ignoring for over four years, the craving to be made love to was grow-ing.

Sexual temptation was a wicked thing. Dark and powerful and primitive. It was not swayed by reason, or pride. It was fed by need, and fanned by desire. She wanted Kane's body inside her much more than Dora's roast dinner.

She wanted him in ways that she'd never wanted Lyall.

So what are you going to do about it, Jessie? she asked herself bluntly as she went through the motions of giving her daughter a bath.

'Mummy,' Emily said as Jessie massaged the no-tears shampoo through her thick curls.

'Mmm?' Jessie murmured a bit blankly. Her mind was elsewhere, after all.

'I like Kane. He's nice.'

'Yes, yes, he is.'

'Do you like him, Mummy?'

'I…well…I…'

'He likes you.'

Jessie sighed. No point in trying to pull the wool over Emily's eyes. Or in lying. Not if she eventually gave in and went out with Kane on Friday night.

'Yes,' she said simply. 'I think perhaps he does.'

Jessie waited for the next question. But none came. Emily just sat there in silence.

Jessie bent down to see the expression on her daughter's face. But it carried that brilliantly blank look which her daughter could adopt when she wanted to hide her feelings from her mother.

'Emily Denton, what are you thinking?' Jessie demanded to know.

'Nothing.'

'Don't lie to me. Tell.'

'I was thinking about Christmas, Mummy. Does Santa *always* give you what you ask for?'

Jessie was glad of this change of subject. 'He does, if you're a good girl.'

'*I'm* a good girl.'

Jessie smiled and gave her daughter a kiss and a cuddle. 'You surely are. You have nothing to worry about, sweetie. Come Christmas Day, you're going to get absolutely *everything* you asked for.'

CHAPTER NINE

JESSIE should have predicted that Kane would charm both Dora and Emily to the degree he did. The man was a charmer through and through. By the time she and Emily returned to the main part of the house for dinner, he had Dora eating out of his hand.

As for Emily...Santa Claus himself couldn't have caused more excitement in the child. She insisted on sitting next to Kane, who treated her as no one had ever treated her before. As if she was a special little princess whose every word was precious and every wish immediately catered to.

Any worry Jessie harboured over her daughter growing too attached to a man who would only be a temporary part of her life was momentarily pushed aside when she saw how happy Emily was. When it was time for her to go to bed—way past her usual time—Emily begged Kane to read her a bedtime story. Which he duly did, and very well too.

Naturally, when the first story was finished, Emily begged for more. A family trait, Jessie decided bitterly, always wanting more.

Kane read her another story, then another, till Emily's yawns finally stopped and she fell asleep.

'She's dropped off,' Jessie said from where she'd been standing in the bedroom doorway with her arms crossed, watching Kane's performance with swiftly returning cynicism. 'You can stop reading now.'

He looked up from the book. 'But I need to find out if Willie Wombat finds his long-lost father,' he protested with a mischievous gleam in his eyes and the most charming smile.

Jessie steeled her heart and rolled her eyes. 'Fine. You take Willie Wombat out into the living room and finish the story whilst I tuck Emily in. I'll be with you shortly to see you out.'

'What, no nightcap?'

'No. It's late and I have to go to work tomorrow. You do too.'

'I'm the boss. I can come in late.'

'Well, I can't. I'm on probation for three months.'

'Who says?'

'Michele. Apparently, that's Harry Wilde's hiring rule. If a new employee can't cut the mustard in three months, he or she gets their walking papers.'

'Harry never told me that. There again, I don't think he expected me to have to do any hiring during the month he was away. Does the idea of probation worry you, Jessie?'

'No. I can cut the mustard. No problem.'

'I'll just bet you can.'

He stood up from where he'd been sitting on the side of Emily's bed, glancing over at the other bed as he made his way towards the door.

Jessie was eminently grateful that she shared a room with her daughter. Also that her own bed, like Emily's, was nicely single. It eliminated temptation.

Jessie stepped aside to let him through the doorway.

'Don't make yourself too comfortable,' she warned drily. 'I won't be long.'

He didn't answer, just gave her a searching look as he moved past.

Jessie wished she'd shut her mouth. Saying too much was almost as bad as saying too little.

She hadn't done much talking during the roast-lamb dinner. Dora and Emily had done enough. And Kane, of course. Brother, could that man talk.

The trouble was he was so darned interesting. And entertaining. Yet, in retrospect, he hadn't actually talked about himself, an unusual trait for a man. His concentration had mostly been on Emily and Dora.

Dora must have told him her whole life story during the course of the meal, from her childhood to her childless marriage to her husband's death, then her recent years of looking after her increasingly fragile widowed mother. She had even revealed how much she resented her younger brother's not having helped with their mother, something she hadn't even told Jessie.

Kane had made all the right noises at the appropriate places. He had a knack with sympathetic murmurs, that was for sure.

Emily had tried to outdo Dora, giving Kane a minute-by-minute description of everything she did every day, pausing for words of praise at intervals, which she duly got.

Jessie smiled wryly down at her daughter as she tucked the sheet around her. Cheeky little devil. A right little flirt too, fluttering her long eyelashes up at Kane all the time.

Jessie had steadfastly not fluttered or flattered or flirted with the man in any way all evening. But despite her keeping a safe distance, he'd still got to her. A quiet look here. A smile there.

Oh, yes, he'd got to her. Made her want things she hated herself for wanting. Not just sex. But more. Too much more.

He was the devil in disguise, tempting her, tormenting her. She knew she should resist him, but feared she was fighting a losing battle. All she could salvage was a bit of pride by not making her surrender too easy. Jessie suspected that Kane Marshall had always found winning much too easy. It would do him good to work for her conquest, such as it would be. Nothing special to him. Just another bit of skirt. Another notch on his gun.

Jessie wondered how many women there'd been since he'd split with his wife. She resolved to never let him know he was the first man she'd even looked at since Lyall, let alone wanted this badly.

'All finished,' she said brusquely as she marched from the bedroom into the living room. 'Let's go.'

He was sitting on the sofa, the one that ran along the wall opposite the television. It was a very roomy sofa. His suit jacket, she noted, had been removed and was draped over one of the kitchen chairs. His tie was there as well, and the top button of his business shirt was undone.

Clearly, he had seduction on his mind, not leaving.

A tremor raced through Jessie.

'You have a very intelligent little girl,' he said as he snapped shut the book he'd been flicking through, placed it on the side-table next to the sofa and stood up. 'Very sweet, too,' he added.

'Unlike her mother,' Jessie snapped, once again folding her arms across her chest.

'Oh, I suspect the mother could be even sweeter than the daughter,' he said as he walked slowly towards her, bypassing the chair with the jacket and tie. 'In the right circumstances.'

'Don't you dare touch me,' she warned when he was less than an arm-length away.

She was standing in the middle of the kitchenette, with her back not far from the kitchen sink.

He stopped and frowned at her. 'You do realise you are being ridiculous,' he said softly.

Was she?

Possibly. But she wasn't about to back down.

'I will not have sex with you with my daughter sleeping in the next room.'

His eyebrows lifted. 'Sex was not what I had in mind for now, Jessie. Just a kiss. Or two.'

'Huh! Men like you don't stop at a kiss or two.'

He frowned. 'Men like me,' he murmured. 'Now, I wonder what you mean by that? Presumably nothing very complimentary. I suspect you've already lumped me in with the type of divorced guy who wants to sow his wild oats, with no strings attached. Or perhaps the sleazebags you told me about who target single mothers because they think they're desperates. Am I right?'

'Something like that.'

'You're wrong. I'm nothing like that at all.'

'I only have your word for that.'

'I haven't been with a woman since my divorce,' he shocked her by saying. 'Natalie was the last woman I slept with.'

Jessie blinked. It was over a year since he'd left his wife! It didn't seem possible. A man like him, so handsome and virile-looking. Women would have been throwing themselves at him all the time.

'But why? Are you seriously undersexed or something?'

He laughed. 'You wish.'

'But…but…'

'Look, I guess after the failure of my marriage I became a bit wary, and very selective. Casual sex held little appeal. I wanted a real relationship with an intelligent woman who wanted the same things I wanted.'

A career woman, she interpreted that to mean. One who'd give him company and sex, but not expect him to fulfill the traditional roles as husband and father of her children.

Jessie couldn't see a single mother with a demanding four-year-old filling those requirements. Not on a permanent basis.

'Then last Friday night,' he went on, 'I was hit by a thunderbolt. You. Suddenly, I didn't care what you were or who you were. I just had to have you. Be with you. Make mad, passionate love to you.'

She looked away from his eyes, lest he see the same crazy compulsion in hers. He reached out to turn her face back to the front again, his fingers both gentle and possessive. Her arms—suddenly heavy—slipped out of their crossed mode to hang loosely by her sides.

'You want that too, Jessie,' he whispered. 'Don't deny it. I've seen the desire in your eyes. And the fear. You think I'll hurt you. You and Emily. But I won't. I promise. I'd cut out my heart before I did anything to hurt either of you. I can see how special you are together. More special than any mother and daughter I have ever known. I want only good things for you both. Trust me. I'm one of the good guys. Now kiss me, Jessie Denton.'

She didn't kiss him. Because he kissed her first, cupping her face and taking her mouth with his, not waiting long before prying her lips open and sending his tongue to meet hers. The contact was electric, firing a heat that raced through her veins and skin, spreading like a bushfire raging out of control. Her arms rose of their own accord to slide around his body, her palms cementing themselves to his back as she pulled him closer. Then closer still.

He moaned deep in his throat, the sound an echo of what was going through her own head. The yearning for even closer contact was acute, but they couldn't be any closer if they tried. They were already glued together, mouth to mouth, chest to chest, stomach to stomach, thigh to thigh.

The anticipation of how he would feel, filling her to the utmost, took Jessie's breath away. If only she wasn't wearing jeans. A skirt could have been lifted, panties thrust aside. They could have done it right there and then, standing up. She'd never done it like that, standing up. She'd never even thought about it before.

She thought about it now and literally went weak at the knees. Did he feel her falling? Was that why he pushed her back up against the sink, to stop her from falling to the floor?

Jessie instinctively shifted her legs apart, giving him better access. His hips moved against her, the friction exquisite. Soon, she was moaning with abject need and total surrender.

'Mummy!'

Emily's high wail cut through Jessie's near-orgasmic state, bringing her back to earth with a crash.

'Oh, God,' she moaned, wrenching her mouth away from his. 'Emily.'

The mother in her, she swiftly realised, was still stronger than the woman, even the wanton woman Kane had so swiftly reduced her to. In another second or two, she would have been practically screaming. Disgusted with herself, she squeezed out from behind Kane's heaving chest, leaving him to sag against the sink whilst she dashed into the bedroom.

'What is it, Emily?' she asked in a voice that mocked what was still going on inside her. So calm-sounding.

'I had a bad dream,' Emily whimpered. 'There was a bear. A big one. I was scared.'

Bears often figured in Emily's nightmares. Jessie sometimes wished there weren't so many children's stories with bears in them.

'There are no bears living in Australia,' Jessie explained gently for the umpteenth time. 'Except in the zoo. You don't have to be scared about bears.'

'Is Kane still here?' Emily asked fretfully.

'Yes. Why?'

'He won't let the bear get me. He'll chase it away.'

Jessie rolled her eyes. 'Fine. You don't have to worry about any bears then, do you? So go back to sleep now,' she crooned, gently stroking her daughter's head. 'OK?'

Emily yawned. 'OK.' She closed her eyes and was back fast asleep in no time.

Jessie envied her child that ability. Sometimes, Emily would fall asleep as soon as her head hit the pillow. Jessie had never been a good sleeper, finding it difficult to shut her mind down at night. She knew she would do more than her fair share of tossing and turning tonight.

But it was clear that to continue fighting her feelings for Kane was futile. And rather ridiculous. He was right when he'd said that. They were adults. They wanted each other. OK, so she probably wanted more from Kane than he wanted from her but that was always going to be the case. She was a woman and he was a man.

Jessie had always been a reasonably decisive person, unlike her mother, who'd muddled through most of the events that had shaped her and Jessie's lives. When she was growing up, taking charge of her own life had been one of Jessie's main goals. Mostly, she'd been successful. In hindsight, Lyall had been a big error in judgement, but the consequences of her mistake had led to great joy.

Getting involved with Kane was possibly unwise. But at the same time she was only human, not a saint.

Having tucked Emily in once more, she returned to the living room, determined not to muddle through.

She was surprised to find Kane putting on his jacket.

He turned with a troubled expression on his face. 'I'm sorry, Jessie,' he said, stuffing his tie into one of the pockets. 'I didn't mean for things to go that far. I really didn't. But you do have an unfortunate effect on me.'

Jessie frowned. 'Unfortunate?'

Kane smiled a wry smile. 'I'm not used to losing control. I pride myself on being a planner. I rarely go off at half-cock.'

She couldn't help laughing, although she smothered it so as not to risk waking Emily.

'Yes, well, if I had actually *gone* off at half-cock,' he muttered, 'I might be able to laugh too.'

'Oh,' she said, taken aback by this revelation. 'I thought…'

'No,' he growled. 'I didn't.'

'It must have been a darned close call.'

'Agonisingly so.'

'Could you wait till Friday night, do you think?'

His eyes flared wide. 'Do you mean what I think you mean?'

'I would imagine so.'

His face actually lit up. 'Wow. That's a turn-up for the books.'

'I decided you were right. I was being ridiculous.

But I want you to understand that this can't really go anywhere. I'm not the woman you're looking for, Kane. I have Emily for starters. And a full-time job now. At best, I could be your friend and part-time lover.' There! She'd taken charge and it felt good.

He didn't say a single word for a few seconds, just let his eyes search her face. She could not tell what he hoped to find.

'I can handle that,' he said at last.

Jessie wished she knew what he was thinking. And planning. He'd just told her he was a planner. Something in his voice and his face suggested his agenda wasn't quite the same as hers.

But what?

She hoped he wasn't underestimating her. Or thinking she was a push-over after all.

Time for some more taking charge.

'By the way, on Friday,' she said firmly, 'I won't be staying anywhere with you all night, so don't go thinking I will. You have from seven till midnight. I can't expect Dora to mind Emily later than that. She's an old lady.'

'I could pay for a baby-sitter,' he suggested.

'Someone I don't know? No way, José. It's Dora, or nobody.'

'Fine. I won't argue. But I think you're in danger of becoming an over-protective mother.'

'Think what you like. It won't change my attitude towards my daughter.'

'I never thought it would. But that's OK. I admire a woman who knows her own mind.'

'And I admire a man who respects a woman's wishes.'

'I'll remember that.'

Yes, but for how long? Jessie wondered.

Till Friday night, naturally. That was the aim of this game after all. Get the girl into bed. But after that, Kane might not be quite so accommodating.

Still, she would cross that bridge when she came to it.

Till then, she was going to have a hard job thinking about anything but Friday night.

CHAPTER TEN

A COPY of a book called *Winning at Work* was sitting on Jessie's desk when she got in the next morning.

'Is this from you?' she asked Michele, who was already there at her desk, beavering away.

'Nope. It was there when I got in. I imagine Kane dropped it off for you to have a look at.'

Jessie recalled he'd said something about a book.

She picked it up and turned it over, blinking at the sight of Kane's photo on the back.

'Good lord!' she exclaimed. 'He's the author!'

Michele glanced up with a surprised look on her attractive face. 'You mean you didn't know the man who drove you home yesterday was *the* Kane Marshall, management guru and motivator extraordinaire?'

'No! I've never heard of *the* Kane Marshall.' Other than his being the twin brother of Curtis Marshall, possible philanderer.

'Something tells me that's about to change,' Michele muttered under her breath.

'He actually *wrote* this?' Jessie said, still stunned.

'Sure did. I gather it's been a runaway best-seller in the USA. It hasn't come out here yet. We Aussies aren't into self-help books as much as the Americans. But we're getting there.'

'Have you read it?'

'Nope.'

Jessie stared at the bio inside the front cover. Kane had a list of professional credits a mile long. Degrees in business and marketing. *And* a degree in psychology. This was his first book, but he was apparently well-known in the business world for his weekend seminars called 'Solving Work Problems'. He was described as a gifted after-dinner speaker, with his services being highly sought after by companies as a consultant and an educator.

Jessie sighed. Any secret hope she'd been harbouring that Kane Marshall might change his mind about what kind of woman he was looking to have that real relationship with just went out the window. He was a workaholic!

'You sound tired,' Michele said. 'Late night?'

'No. Just not enough sleep.'

'Aah. Man trouble.'

'What?'

'When a mother can't sleep it has to be man trouble. And it doesn't take much to guess which man. Although I'm not sure what the problem is. Do you already have a boyfriend? Is that it?'

'Goodness, no, I haven't had a boyfriend since Emily's father.' She and Michele had chatted a bit about their backgrounds over coffee yesterday, so Michele knew about Lyall.

'Aah…' Michele nodded. 'The once-bitten, twice-shy syndrome.'

'Can you blame me? After Lyall died, I found out he wasn't just two-timing me. He was triple-timing me.'

'Not nice,' Michele agreed. 'But that was Lyall, not Kane.'

'Maybe, but in some ways they're alike. Both tall, dark and handsome, with great smiles and the gift of the gab. Those sort of guys are hard to trust.'

'So you didn't say yes when he asked you out?' Michele ventured.

Jessie sighed. 'Yes. I did. We're on for Friday night,' she confessed.

'Playing hard to get, I see. Smart girl.'

'You call that playing hard to get?' Jessie put Kane's book down on her part of the work station and pulled out her chair.

'Sure. That's five whole days since you met him.'

Jessie sank down into her chair. 'Actually, it will be a week since I met him.'

Michele's eyes widened. 'Really? You'd met him before the interview on Monday?'

'Yes. In a bar in town last Friday night. But we didn't exchange names. I—er—drank with him and danced with him, but I did a flit when he wanted more than dancing. He was as shocked as I was when I showed up here yesterday.'

'Shocked, but still pleased. He's obviously very taken with you, Jessie.'

'You think so? It's hard to tell with men. It could just be sex, you know.'

'Nothing wrong with that. Lots of relationships start with sex. Don't fall into the trap of being too cynical about men, Jessie. There are some genuinely good ones out there. I don't know Kane all that well, but what I know I like. Everyone here thinks he's great. So give him a chance. Oh, and don't forget to go thank him for the book. He'll be dying to know what you think, I'll bet. Lunch-time would be a good time, when Karen's out. She and Margaret have lunch together at a café up the road every day at one. Kane has his lunch delivered, Margaret tells me. He's an obsessive reader and usually stays at his desk. You could pop along any time after one and he'd be all alone.'

'Are you sure that's a good idea?'

'Why not? What do you think he's going to do? Ravish you on his desk?'

Jessie didn't like to admit that that was exactly what she thought he might do. Worse was the reality that she wouldn't mind one bit.

She'd already come into work wearing a skirt, instead of jeans. And no stockings.

The clear blue sky this morning had promised a hot summer's day, so her selection of a pink and white floral wrap-around skirt, a simple pink T-shirt and slip-on white sandals was really quite an appropriate outfit for work. No one could have guessed by just looking at her that whilst she'd dressed she'd secretly thrilled to the thought of how accessible she was, if by some chance Kane found the time and the place to seduce her at work.

Stupid fantasy, really. But darned exciting to think about.

By lunch-time, every nerve-ending in Jessie's body was tap-dancing. She was grateful when Michele left to do some shopping. A trip to the ladies' room assured her that her make-up was still in place. She wouldn't have been surprised if it had melted all over her face. But she looked OK. Her hair was up, secured by a long pink clip. She toyed with taking it down, then decided that would be on the obvious side. The last thing she wanted was to be obvious.

Thankfully she had a good excuse for going to his office. She didn't want to show up looking like a desperate. Even if she was fast becoming one.

Another attack of nerves sent her bolting into a toilet cubicle. Five minutes later, she was back at her desk, where she skip-read a few chapters of the book to get the gist of it whilst she stuffed down one of the two sandwiches she'd brought from home. That done, she made her way to Kane's office. It was one-twenty.

Karen's desk was blessedly empty. Fate hadn't made her stay back for some reason. Jessie's heart sank, however, when she saw the door to the inner office was half open and a woman's voice was emerging.

Don't tell me Karen is in there with him, she thought.

Jessie took a couple of steps towards the door, grinding to a halt when the woman—who didn't sound like Karen—said something about being pregnant.

'Pregnant!' Kane exclaimed in a shocked voice. 'Good God, Natalie.'

Jessie sucked in sharply. Natalie. That was his ex-wife's name.

'Don't worry, darling,' the woman said in a droll

tone. 'It's not yours. I'm only a month gone and it's at least a couple of months since we were together. Besides, if I recall rightly, you used a condom.'

Jessie's heart squeezed tight. A couple of months ago Kane had still been sleeping with his ex. Yet he'd made her think he'd been celibate since they split up over a year ago. She'd thought at the time that was unlikely. What other women had he lied to her about?

'Who's the father?' she heard Kane ask.

'Some guy I met at a party. A lawyer. I didn't even find out his last name, would you believe? But I could find it out if I want to.'

'What are you going to do about the baby?'

'I know you'll think I'm mad, but I'm going to have it.'

'You're joking!'

'No. No, Kane, I'm not.'

Jessie couldn't bear to stand there, listening to any more of this conversation. She turned and fled back down the corridor as quietly as her pounding heart would permit. Tears threatened, but she made it back to the toilet cubicle, dry-eyed. Even then, strangely, she didn't cry. She wanted to, but something inside her was damming back the tears, a big, cold, angry lump.

One part of her wanted to go back and confront him, throw his lies in his face. But another part of her argued that to do that was to finish it between them.

Could she bear that? To walk away without going to bed with him, at least once?

Jessie supposed she could. She could do just about anything once she put her mind to it.

But it would be hard, especially with his being here at work every day. She would keep running into him. And wanting him.

So, no, she wouldn't be confronting him, Jessie decided as she made her way back to her desk. Or accusing him. She would use him as he was using her. For sex.

At least this added knowledge of his character would stop her from falling in love with him. The man was a lying scumbag, like most men. An empty charmer. Just because he'd made a raging success of his professional life didn't make him a good guy, as he claimed to be.

When she thought about his choice of career it suited him very well. What was he, really, but a glorified salesman? A con artist. A seller of dreams. Such seminars as he conducted preyed on people's weaknesses, making them think they could be winners too, if only they listened to him. He'd spin her a whole world of dreams too, if she let him.

But she wasn't going to let him. Or listen to him. He could talk all the bulldust he liked. None of it was going to get to her any more.

'What are you muttering to yourself about?'

His voice behind her came out of the blue, startling her.

Jessie swallowed, then spun slowly round on her office chair, a cool smile at the ready.

'Just thinking of all the things I have to do before

Christmas,' she said, her eyes running over the man himself for the first time that day.

Yes, he *was* gorgeous. Utterly. With that air of masculine confidence which she found almost irresistible.

But she was ready for him now, ready and armed with the knowledge of his true self.

'I did offer to take you shopping,' he said with one of his winning smiles.

'So you did. And I might have to take you up on that by this time next week.'

'What about this Saturday? Emily could come with us. I promise I'll have a proper car seat by then.'

Jessie found her own smile. A slow smile. A saucy smile. 'Do you think you'll be capable of getting out of bed after Friday night?'

His blue eyes registered shock. But then he smiled back. 'Is that a challenge of some sort?'

'Let's just say it's been a while for me. I might take some satisfying.'

A flicker of a frown skittered across his face. 'Boy, when you decide to do something you do it full throttle, don't you?'

'I have a take-no-prisoners attitude to life sometimes.'

'That's what I like about you. You're so damned honest and upfront. Except when you're cruising bars looking for straying hubbies, that is,' he added ruefully.

Jessie shrugged. 'That's all in the past now that I have a decent job. And it's not as though most of those guys didn't deserve to get caught. So tell me, Kane, were you ever unfaithful to your wife?'

'What a question!'

'One you don't want to answer, I see.'

'No, I don't mind answering it. I was never unfaithful. I sowed my wild oats plenty in my younger years. Once I got married, however, I put all that behind me.'

'One of the good guys,' she said just a fraction tartly.

He frowned. 'I take it you're still not convinced.'

'Does it matter?'

'It matters to me.'

Jessie decided this conversation was running off the rails. 'By the way, thank you for your book. I was suitably impressed. And a little surprised. I didn't realise you were famous.'

'I'm not so famous,' he said modestly.

'But you will be. Your book is fabulous.' Jessie knew you could never flatter a man enough. Flattery, she could handle. And flirting. Just no falling in love.

He looked so ridiculously pleased, she felt guilty. 'But you can't possibly have read it yet.'

'Well, not properly. But I will. Before Friday night.'

'Stop talking about Friday night!' he suddenly bit out in an agitated fashion. 'I know it's only three days away, but after last night it seems like an eternity. I don't think I slept a wink.'

He did look tired, now that she came to think of it. There were dark circles under his eyes.

'I didn't sleep very well myself,' she confessed.

'Jessie, this is ridiculous. Why should we torture ourselves? Be with me tonight. Get Dora to mind Emily. She told me last night that she'd be quite happy to mind Emily any night we wanted to go out. I asked her. I even offered to pay her but she refused. She said she'd be happy to do it any time.'

Jessie felt both flustered and furious. 'You had no right to go behind my back like that.'

'No right to do what?' he countered. 'Try to organise things so that I can spend some time with a woman I'm crazy about?'

Jessie flushed at the passion in his voice. 'I told you. I don't like to be rushed.'

His sigh was ragged. 'OK. Yes, I am rushing you. I'm sorry. It's just that life is so short and when you see something that you really want, you have to reach out and grab it before something happens and it gets away from you.'

'Is that what you tell people in your book?'

'Not that I recall. This is something which has come upon me just lately. It's possibly worse today.'

'Why is it worse today?'

'Would you believe my ex-wife has just been in to see me? And guess what? She's pregnant, by some guy she doesn't even know the name of. *And* she's going to keep the baby.' Kane shook his head in utter bewilderment.

'What's wrong with that?' Jessie challenged. For pity's sake, did he expect her to have an abortion? He'd divorced her because she wanted children. The man just didn't understand how strong the maternal impulse could be. She could never have terminated *her* baby, and she hadn't even been craving one at the time.

'You don't know Natalie,' he muttered. 'She's not the single-mother type.'

'Is there a single-mother type?'

'No. I guess not. It was just so unexpected, not to mention quick. Our divorce papers only came through three months ago. You can imagine how I felt when she announced she was pregnant.'

Actually, Jessie didn't have to imagine anything. She'd been there and heard his reaction. He'd been worried sick that it was *his*.

'It's not as though you're still in love with her,' Jessie said impatiently. '*Are* you?'

'No, of course not!'

'Then her having another man's baby is irrelevant. Leave her to her life and you get on with yours.'

He stared at her for a second before his mouth broke into a wry grin. 'Yes, Dr Denton. I'll do just that. Which brings me back to tonight. What do you say, Jessie? Would you let me take you out to dinner? Just dinner.'

That was about as believable as 'the cheque's in the post'!

Jessie scooped in a deep breath whilst every pore in her screamed at her to agree. But to say yes would be the kiss of death. She'd show her weakness and then he'd have her right where he wanted her.

'I'm sorry, Kane,' she said, quite truthfully. 'I make it a policy never to go out during the week. You'll just have to wait. You can always have a lot of cold showers,' she suggested with more than a hint of malice.

Their eyes met, and held.

'I don't think there's enough cold water in the world to fix my problem,' he bit out. 'Still, I guess I'll survive. But I would suggest that if you're going to come into work each day looking good enough to eat, then for pity's sake, keep well out of my way!'

CHAPTER ELEVEN

'MUMMY'S got a boyfriend! Mummy's got a boy-friend! Mummy's got a...'

'Yes, all right, Emily,' Jessie interrupted sharply. 'I've heard you. And do stop jumping up and down on your bed. It's not a trampoline. Look, go and put a video on. I'll never be ready in time if you keep distracting me.'

Emily was off the bed and out of the room in a flash. If there was one thing that would successfully shut Emily up, it was watching one of her favourite videos.

Being left alone, however, didn't help Jessie as much as she had hoped. Her hands kept shaking for starters, and her usually decisive mind could not seem to settle on what she should wear tonight.

Kane had told her in an email yesterday—one of several he'd sent her during the last three days—that she didn't need to be dressed up. Something casual would be fine.

Jessie had been relieved at the time. Her wardrobe was ninety-five per cent casual. But most were on the cheap side.

The evening promised to be warm, so a skirt was probably a good choice. She pulled out a black and white one similar to the pink floral she'd worn to work the other day, the one which Kane had said made her look good enough to eat.

Oh, dear. She shouldn't have thought about that. Her nipples tightened and a little tremor ran down the back of her legs.

A glance at her watch brought instant panic. She only had a quarter of an hour before Kane was due to pick her up at seven. She'd already showered and done her make-up since arriving home, but she was still naked under her robe, her hair was a mess and Dora would be arriving any moment with Emily's dinner.

The darling woman had promised to feed the child, as well as look after her for the night. She seemed just as excited at Jessie having a so-called boyfriend as Emily was. Jessie hadn't liked to disillusion them over Kane's true intentions—they both thought he was the ant's pants—so she let them think what they liked.

Meanwhile, Jessie just kept telling herself that tonight was nothing serious. Just fun and games.

'Fun and games,' she repeated as she opened her underwear drawer and pulled out a black satin bra and matching G-string from underneath her more sensible sets. They had been outrageously expensive when she'd bought them pre-Emily, and had rarely been worn. Motherhood had made her breasts larger, so when she put the bra on, her cups really did runneth over.

But oh, my, she did look seriously sexy, with a cleavage deeper than the Grand Canyon. The G-string looked OK from the front. But she didn't even risk a peek at a rear view. What she didn't know couldn't depress her.

A knock on the granny-flat door was followed by Dora's voice as she opened the door and came in. 'It's just me, Jessie, with Em's dinner.'

'I'm still not ready, Dora. Can you organise things out there for a few minutes?'

'No worries. We'll be fine, won't we, Emily?'

No reply from Emily.

'Emily,' her mother shouted whilst she manoeuvred on the stretchy black cross-over top she'd bought to go with the skirt. 'Sit up at the table for Dora. I've set a place for her, Dora. And her apple juice is in her special cup in the fridge.'

'Yes, yes, stop fussing. I can manage. You get on with getting ready. Kane will be here soon, you know.'

'I know,' Jessie muttered, hurriedly wrapping the skirt around her hips and tying the sash tightly at the back. One thing motherhood hadn't improved on her figure was her waistline. It was slightly thicker now. Still, her bigger bust and hips balanced that, so the overall look was still hourglass.

Reasonably satisfied with the result—the amount of flesh she had on display in the deep V-neckline gave her a few butterflies—Jessie turned to doing something with her hair, which was a bit of a frizz, due to the humidity in the air. The only thing for it was up, of course. So up it went, brushed back from her face quite brutally and anchored to her crown with a black scrunchie.

Naturally, quite a few strands and curls escaped

but guys had always told her they liked that. They said it looked sexy. And sexy was definitely the look she was aiming for tonight.

Her jewelry she kept to a minimum. A silver chain locket necklace and silver loop earrings. Her perfume was an expensive one, a present from Dora for her birthday back in June. It was called True Love.

True irony, Jessie thought wryly as she slipped her feet into the same strappy black high heels she'd worn the previous Friday. Her only regret about her appearance was that she hadn't invested in some fake tan. No sleeves and no stockings meant that a lot of her pale flesh was on display. But she hadn't been paid yet and could have only afforded the cheap variety. Better to have no tan than to have orange streaks and oddly coloured elbows and ankles.

'Kane's here,' Dora chimed out a few seconds before he knocked on the door. She must have heard his footsteps on the concrete path which led around to the granny flat.

'Coming,' Jessie replied, amazed at how nauseous she was suddenly feeling. What had happened to the carefree girl she'd used to be?

Well, that girl was gone, Jessie realised, replaced by a nervous wreck who was scared stiff that she'd be so hopeless that Kane wouldn't want to see her again after tonight. Which might be for the best. But somehow, at this precise moment, wisdom wasn't Jessie's long suit.

Thinking about the girl she had used to be, however, reminded her that she didn't have any condoms. Still, she was sure Kane would be well prepared. A man who didn't want children would *always* be prepared.

'Kane! Kane!' Emily's excited voice reached Jessie.

Jessie hoped her daughter didn't start chanting to him about his being her mummy's boyfriend.

'Won't be a sec,' she called out from the bedroom as she hurriedly put her make-up, brush and wallet into her black patent evening bag and headed for the bedroom door.

Kane hadn't actually come inside. He'd stayed standing on the back doorstep under the light that shone down from above.

'Oh,' she said on seeing him. 'We're colour co-ordinated.'

He was wearing a black suit—casually tailored—with a white T-shirt underneath. No doubt a very expensive designer white T-shirt. Not that it mattered. On him, anything looked good.

By the look in his eyes what she was wearing was meeting with *his* approval as well. It was good that men rarely knew what a woman's clothes cost. She wouldn't mind betting that his T-shirt had cost more than her whole outfit. Minus the lingerie and the shoes, of course. They *had* been expensive.

'Doesn't Mummy look pretty?' Emily said from where Dora, by some miracle, had kept her sitting at the table, eating her dinner. Admittedly, it was spaghetti bolognaise, Emily's favourite. But Jessie had pictured her daughter hurling herself into Kane's arms the moment he arrived.

'Yes, indeed,' Kane agreed with gleaming eyes.

'Are you going to ask Mummy to marry you?'

It was just the sort of question Jessie had feared.

She groaned her embarrassment whilst Dora laughed.

Kane, the suave devil, took it in his stride. 'Would you like me to?' he said.

'Oh, yes,' Emily replied.

'Your wish is my command, princess. The trouble is I don't think your mummy's quite ready to marry *me* yet.'

'Why not?' Emily demanded to know, scowling up at her mother.

'Kane and I have only known each other a week,' Jessie said with more patience than she was feeling. 'You don't marry someone until you've known them much longer than that.'

'Two weeks?' Emily suggested, and both Dora and Kane laughed.

Jessie rolled her eyes. 'At *least* two weeks. Now, you be good for Dora tonight and go to bed when she tells you to. Thanks a bunch, Dora.'

'My pleasure, love. Just you and Kane have a good time. And don't go thinking you have to rush home. Stay out as long as you like. I'll go to sleep on your sofa.'

'I shouldn't be too late,' Jessie said firmly. More for Kane's ears than Dora's. 'Bye, sweetie.' She gave Emily a kiss. 'Love you. See you in the morning.'

'At least two weeks, eh?' Kane said as they walked together along the side-path. 'In that case, we should be engaged by Christmas.'

'Very funny,' Jessie said.

'Who says I'm joking?'

'Kane, *stop* it.'

'Stop what?'

Jessie ground to a halt beside Dora's prized hydrangeas, which were in full bloom. 'Stop being ridiculous. You and I both know you would never marry me.'

'Why not?'

'For one thing I have Emily.'

'I think Emily's fantastic. Cutest kid I've ever met.'

Jessie shook her head in exasperation. 'This is a stupid conversation and I don't want to continue it.'

'Good, because I'm sick of talking, anyway.' Before she could read his intention, he pulled her into his arms and kissed her, right there and then.

Jessie's first instinct was to struggle. What if Dora came out and around the side of the house and saw them? She even opened her mouth to protest.

Silly move.

His tongue darted inside and she didn't think about anything much after that for a full five minutes. By the time he let her come up for air, her head was swimming and her body was on the countdown to lift-off. She actually moaned in dismay when his mouth lifted. Her fingers tightened on what she thought was his back, but was actually her evening bag, resting against his back.

'Now I know what to do with you,' he said thickly as he stroked an erotic finger over her puffy lips. 'Every time you start to get stroppy tonight, I'm going to kiss you. So be warned and try to behave yourself in the restaurant. Unless, of course, you'd rather we didn't go out to eat. We could drive straight to my place if you prefer. I do have food there in my freezer and a perfectly good microwave. Wine too, and fresh fruit. I'm actually quite domesticated. I only turn into a wild beast around you.'

'I like the wild beast,' she heard herself saying in a low, husky voice. But that finger on her lips felt incredible. Before she could think better of it, her tongue-tip came out to meet it. He stared down at her mouth and then slowly, ever so slowly, inserted his finger inside.

Her stomach somersaulted.

'Suck it,' he commanded. And she did, thinking all the while that she would do anything he told her to do tonight.

The thought blew her away. This was dangerous territory she'd just entered. But more exciting than anything she'd ever experienced before. Lyall was kindergarten playtime compared to this man.

His blue eyes narrowed as he watched her blindly obey him.

His tortured groan shocked her, as did the way he reefed his finger out, as if she were a cobra, not a woman on the verge of becoming his sex slave.

'Enough,' he growled. 'You are one contrary woman, Jessie Denton,' he added. 'You run hot and cold all the time. So what is it to be tonight? You decide. The restaurant, or my place?'

Jessie was way beyond hypocrisy. She was as turned on as she knew he was. Any further delay would brand her a tease and she'd never been that.

'Your place,' she said, dropping her arms back to her sides as she took a step back from him.

He didn't reply, just grabbed her free hand and dragged her out to his car as if the hounds of hell were after them.

'Belt up,' he ordered as he fired the engine. 'And no chit-chat. It's not that far to my place at Balmoral but the traffic's heavy going into the city. I need to concentrate.'

Balmoral, she thought, her earlier dazed state slowly receding. An exclusive inner north-shore sub-urb with an equally exclusive beach. She'd been there once to a restaurant on its foreshores. Very up-market. Very pricy. After the recent housing boom, even the simplest apartment there would cost the earth.

She couldn't see Kane having a simple apartment. It would be a sleek bachelor pad with a view and jacuzzi. Or a penthouse, with a pool, leather furniture and a king-size animal-print-covered bed.

She was wrong on both counts. First it was a house, not an apartment. Secondly, it wasn't modern or overtly masculine. It was old—probably built in the thirties—with lots of art deco features and loads of antique furniture. The only thing she was right about was the water-view, which was magnificent from its site up on the side of a hill.

'Did you live here with your wife?' were Jessie's first words after he had led her into the cosy front sitting room. Through the windows she could see the sea down below. And the lights of the restaurant she'd once visited.

'No,' he replied. 'We had an apartment in town. I bought this when we separated. My parents live a couple of streets away. And my brother lives in the next suburb.'

Jessie thought it was nice that he'd chosen to live so close to his family.

'This is not what I expected,' she said.

He smiled. 'I know. That's one reason why I wanted to bring you here. Seeing for yourself is worth a thousand words. I keep telling you I'm not what you think, Jessie. Now, put that infernal bag down and come here…'

Jessie sucked in sharply. She should have known he'd get right down to it, once they were alone. It was what she wanted too. Inside.

But her earlier decision to come here and jump straight into bed with him had been easy when she was still in his arms, with his kisses still hot in her memory and his finger in her mouth. Not quite so easy standing here in his living room with the lights on and nothing but the sound of the sea in the background.

He frowned at her when she didn't move. 'Don't tell me you're nervous. Or that you've changed your mind,' he added darkly.

'No. No, I haven't changed my mind. But yes, I am nervous,' she confessed shakily. 'It's been so long and I…'

'How long?' he broke in.

Jessie was shocked when tears pricked at her eyes. Goodness, what was there to be crying about? 'I…I haven't been with a man since Lyall.'

She was thankful that he didn't act all surprised, or suspicious, over this statement of fact.

'I see,' he said simply, then smiled. A soft, almost loving smile. 'That's wonderful.'

She was the one who was shocked. 'Wonderful? What's wonderful about it? I've probably forgotten how to do it!'

He laughed. 'You haven't forgotten, sweetheart. You're a natural. But if you have,' he said as he walked forward and put her bag down for her, 'you have me to show you how all over again. But *my* way. Not Lyall's way, or any other man's way.'

'And what's your way?' she choked out as he took her hand and started leading her from the room.

The look he threw over his shoulder sent shivers rippling down her spine. 'The way which gives you the most pleasure, of course. I have a plan, as usual. But if at first I don't succeed, then I'll try, try again. You might be amazed at how many times I can make love in five hours.'

'It…it's already half past seven,' Jessie blurted out, trying to stop herself from totally losing it. But dear heaven, he meant to make love to her for the whole five hours?

'So I'll be a little late getting you home,' he said as he drew her through a doorway, switching on a light as he went. 'I'm sure Dora will forgive me.'

The room was, naturally, a bedroom. A huge bedroom with polished wooden floorboards, high ceilings, antique furniture and a wide brass bed covered in a silvery grey satin quilt with matching pillows. The lamps each side of the bed had brass bases with white shades and long fringes. The chandelier over-head was crystal and brass. Lace curtains covered the long windows on the wall adjacent to the bed. In the opposite wall was another door, which was open and led into an *en suite* bathroom. The light shone in just far enough for Jessie to see it was more modern than the rest of the house, being all white. Possibly a re-cent renovation.

It was a beautiful bedroom, only the colour of the bedding betraying that a man slept here, and not a woman.

Although, of course, women could have slept here. With Kane. His ex-wife perhaps. And others Kane had forgotten to mention.

Jessie didn't like that thought.

'What's wrong?' Kane said immediately.

'Nothing,' she lied.

'Come, now, Jessie, don't lie to me. You looked at that bed and something not very nice came into your mind. What was it?'

'I guess I didn't like to think of you having been in there with other women.'

'But I told you. There have been no other women since Natalie.'

'What about Natalie?'

'What about her?'

'You slept with her recently. I know you did. I overheard both of you in the office the other day. I went to thank you for the book at lunch-time that day and you were discussing her pregnancy and she said you weren't to worry, because it wasn't yours.'

Kane stared at her. 'Why didn't you say anything before this?'

'I...I didn't want to.'

'You just kept it to yourself and held it against me. Hell, Jessie, I wish you'd said something.'

'Would it have changed anything? You did sleep with her, didn't you?'

His grimace showed true anguish. 'Look, it was three months ago and only the once. We'd met up in her flat the night our divorce papers came through. She'd offered to cook me dinner as a kind of celebration, to show there were no hard feelings. We had too many glasses of wine over dinner and she said how about it, for old times' sake? If I hadn't been drunk and lonely it would never have happened. I can't tell you how much I regretted it afterwards. So did she, I think. It wasn't even good sex. We were both plastered. I didn't mention it because I didn't want you to think I was one of those guys who get rid of their wives and then keep sleeping with them when they feel like a bit, as a lot do. I'm sorry, Jessie. I wasn't trying to deceive you. I just wanted you to believe me when I said on that first Friday night that I wasn't in the habit of picking up women. You were a one-off, believe me. You still are. I want you, Jessie, more than any woman I've ever known. And I know you want me. Please don't keep finding excuses to push me away.'

Jessie knew he was a good talker. A clever persuader. But there was a sincerity in his voice and his eyes that touched her. Surely, he *had* to be telling the truth.

'You really haven't been with anyone else?' she asked.

'Cross my heart and hope to die.'

'I wouldn't want you to die, Kane,' she murmured, stepping forward and snaking her arms up around his neck. 'I want you very much alive.'

He groaned, his mouth crashing down to take hers in a kiss of mind-blowing hunger. Their tongues met, danced, demanded. Their bodies pressed closer, and closer. Their hips jammed together, then ground against each other.

'No, no, not that again,' he gasped as his mouth burst free from hers. 'I haven't waited the last three days for that.'

Her head was spinning but she concurred wholeheartedly. That was not what she wanted, either. She wanted him naked, and inside her. She wanted it all.

She reached round behind her back to untie the bow.

'No,' he said swiftly. 'Let me…'

Kane started undressing her as no man had ever done in her life. So slowly and sensually, his eyes smouldering with desire, his hands not quite steady. First to be disposed of was her skirt, leaving her standing there before him with nothing below her hips but that skimpy G-string.

'Arms up,' he ordered, then he took her top by its hem and began to peel it upwards over her head.

The action covered her eyes for a second or two, Jessie quivering in her momentary darkness, turned on by the thought of how she must look with her arms up, her face masked, but her body being more

and more exposed to his gaze. She'd never thrilled
to a sex-slave fantasy before but she did so now,
imagining herself having been bought by him, being
a helpless prisoner to his passion, with no other pur-
pose than to be an instrument of pleasure.

Not her own.

Suddenly, her own pleasure seemed irrelevant.
This was all for him. Her lord and master. Her soon-
to-be lover.

Even when her top was thrown away, she kept her
eyes shut, enjoying the sensation of being outside
herself, looking in on what was happening with her
mind. She heard him gasp. In admiration, she hoped.

And then his hands were on her again, still soft,
but just as knowing. He took her G-string off first,
which surprised her. She wobbled a bit when he
picked up first one foot and then the other. She stiffened expectantly when he straightened, sucking in
sharply when one of his hands stroked over her belly.
Her eyes squeezed even more tightly together when
it drifted lower, a startled gasp torn from her throat
when both his hands slid between her thighs. But he
didn't touch her there, just eased her legs apart.

'Yes, like that,' she heard him say.

And then his hands were gone, only to be felt
again on her bra clasp. When it gave way and her
breasts were finally naked before his eyes, she felt
no embarrassment, only the most all-consuming
craving to have them touched.

But he didn't touch them.

'Open your eyes,' he told her forcefully.

Of course she obeyed. How could she not? It was the voice of the master.

Opening her eyes, however, brought a wave of dizziness.

'Watch it,' he said, and grabbed her shoulders to steady her swaying body.

Once she was still, his hands moved up to dispose of the scrunchie, letting her hair tumble in wild disarray around her shoulders.

She had never been so turned on, or so compliant.

'I want you to just stand there like that,' he murmured, 'whilst I get undressed.'

Of course, she thought. What else would I do?

He stripped off his own clothes much faster than he had hers. And he took off everything, displaying the kind of body she'd imagined him to have. Muscly and hard, with not too much body hair, a broad chest and a six-pack stomach.

Jessie tried not to stare when he collected a condom from the bedside chest and drew it on.

But she did lick her very dry bottom lip.

'No, not that either,' he snapped, misinterpreting her action. 'Not yet. Later.'

Whatever you want, she almost said. Whenever you want it.

He walked around her a couple of times, just looking at her, standing there in nothing but her high heels. Only when she was at screaming point did he touch her, coming up close from behind, pushing her hair away from one shoulder and bending his head to kiss her neck, softly at first, then more hungrily.

The wild beast swiftly emerged again, and soon

he was sucking on her throat whilst his hands ran roughly up and down her arms. Her back automatically arched against him, the action lifting her breasts in wanton invitation. This time he obliged, cupping them in his hands and squeezing them together whilst his thumbpads rubbed rather cruelly over the already stiffened nipples.

Sensations shot through her like a series of lightning bolts, sizzling with electricity, leaving her burning with a fire which she knew could only be erased one way.

His mouth covered her ear, hot and heavy with his breathing.

'Don't close your legs,' he commanded on a raw whisper.

And then he took her hands in his and stretched them out in front of her, bending her forward till her fingers reached the nearest brass bedpost.

'Hold on to that,' he advised.

Very good advice. Because she might have fallen otherwise. Or fainted.

No man had ever made love to her like this before, in this position. Jessie's head whirled. But there was little time to think before he was inside her, holding her hips captive whilst he ground into her body.

She had never experienced anything so decadent before. But it felt so delicious this way. Wild and wicked and wonderfully wanton. Her mind swiftly joined her body in quest of nothing but more of the pleasure which was rippling through her entire body. She started rocking back and forth against him, tightening her insides in response to each of his forward thrusts.

'Oh, God,' he groaned. 'Yes, yes, that's it, sweetheart. That's the way.'

He let go of her hips and took hold of each of her nipples with his thumbs and forefingers, squeezing them and pulling them downwards. The combination of sensations was way beyond pleasure. It reached the outer stratosphere.

Jessie cried out, then splintered apart with the most intense orgasm she had ever had. By the time Kane followed her several seconds later, she felt as if she'd fallen into quicksand. She clung on to that bedpost for dear life, knowing that if she let go she would surely sink to the floor.

And then she *was* sinking, but somehow she didn't hit the floor. Instead, Kane scooped her up in his arms. How could he do that? her befuddled mind tried to grasp. He was behind her, deep inside her still throbbing flesh. She could still feel him there. But, no, it seemed he wasn't there any longer. She *was* being carried, and being lain down on top of his bed, his very soft, very comfortable bed. He started stroking her hair and her back and her legs, and that wave of exhaustion which had been hovering at the edges of her mind floated softly down over her. She mumbled something. It might have been 'thank you'. She yawned.

Then everything went black.

CHAPTER TWELVE

KANE returned from his trip to the bathroom to gaze down at Jessie asleep on top of his bed, smiling when he saw that she still had those sexy shoes on her feet. Carefully, slowly, he picked up each foot and removed them. She didn't stir.

He'd read her right. She liked men who took charge in the bedroom, who treated her to a bit of caveman style. Yet Kane had never acted quite like that with a female before. Natalie had been of the ilk who, ultimately, liked to be on top. To begin with, he'd liked the fact he didn't have to work hard for his sex. Time and familiarity, however, had eventually dulled his desire for her. Lack of love too, Kane realised. Resentment had built up over her unwillingness to have his children and by the end he hadn't been interested in pleasing her.

He wanted to please Jessie Denton more than any woman he'd ever met. Of course, that was because he'd fallen in love with her. Deeply. Truly. It wasn't just lust. Or fool's love, as he called it. He'd been there, done that, and he knew the difference. He wanted her, not just as his lover but also as his wife and the mother of his children. He might have only known her a week, but he was surer of that than he had been of anything in his life.

He suspected she felt pretty strongly about him,

too. But she was wary after her experience with that scumbag, Lyall. Cynicism was stopping her from seeing he was sincere.

Pity about her overhearing him with Natalie like that. She must have thought him a callous liar. But despite that she'd agreed to come out with him, something she hadn't done in years. His male ego had been very flattered when she'd told him he was the first man she'd been with since Emily's father. His love for her had grown at the news she didn't sleep around. As had his respect. She had character, did Jessie Denton. A tremor ran down Kane's spine as he recalled the force of her orgasm.

He couldn't wait for her to wake up. He was already hard again.

Why *should* you wait? spoke up the caveman still lurking inside him. She wouldn't want to sleep the evening through. If you want her, wake her, take her. Go to it, tiger!

Kane didn't hesitate. He hurried over to the top drawer of the bedside chest, where he'd dropped a newly opened box of condoms earlier that day. Twenty seconds later, he stretched himself out beside her still unconscious form and began trailing his fingers up and down her spine.

Jessie surfaced to consciousness with a shiver of pleasure. Yet it took quite a few seconds for awareness of where she was and what had happened earlier on to strike.

Oh, dear, she thought, grimacing into the pillow. Thankfully she was lying face down. It gave her some extra moments to compose herself before she had to admit she was awake.

Though maybe she wouldn't. Maybe she'd just lie there and pretend she wasn't really awake, just stirring in her sleep. But then that hand, which was sending shivers up and down her spine, moved into territory that jackknifed her over.

'Don't do that!' she gasped.

He smiled, then slid that devilish hand back between her legs. 'Glad to see you've rejoined the living,' he said as he teased her with a fingertip.

She flushed, then gasped when he lightly grazed over her exquisitely swollen peak. 'You're not a good guy at all,' she said breathlessly. 'You're wicked.'

His smile broadened. 'I'll take that as a compliment. Do you want to be on top this time?'

Her mouth fell open as she stared up at him. She had never been with a man who was so forthright, or so...so...

'No? That's OK. Next time, perhaps.' And he bent his head to her nearest nipple. At the same time that tantalising finger stopped what it was doing to delve further into her.

Jessie's mind was torn between two sources of pleasure. His mouth on her breast, licking, sucking, nibbling. But it was what was happening inside her which had her breathing really hard. Her belly began to tighten and she thought she would warn him.

'I...I'm going to come,' she blurted out.

He lifted his head and smiled. 'That's good. Now, are you sure you don't want to be on top?'

It must have been a rhetorical question because before she knew it, he'd hauled her up to be straddling him.

'Now take me in your hands and just ease me inside you as you sink down,' he instructed, sensing perhaps that she'd never done it like this before either. Jessie realised that she'd had a rather boring sex life up till now. Lyall had been forceful in bed but selfish, she realised. Her other boyfriends had just been ignorant. Only her natural love of being kissed and caressed and, yes, penetrated had made those sexual encounters pleasurable.

She took Kane in her hands. Just the thought of putting him inside her body with her own hands was so exciting.

Suddenly, shyness wasn't an option.

'Hey,' he said when her fingers enclosed tight around him. 'Gently does it.'

She didn't even blush. She was too focused on feeling his beautiful hardness, then inserting him deep into her eagerly accepting flesh. And ooh…it felt as good as she had known it would. No further instructions were needed, though he did take hold of her hips when she began to ride him. Probably to slow her down. The urge to go faster and faster was almost unbearable. Her need for release was intense.

'Yes!' she cried out when the first spasm hit.

He must have come, too. She vaguely recalled his own raw groan of release whilst she was moaning and groaning. When she finally collapsed across him, his arms enclosed her, very tenderly, she thought.

This time, she didn't fall asleep. She didn't feel tired at all. Just blissfully at peace. And incredibly happy.

When he eventually rolled her over and eased himself out of her body, she actually whimpered in protest. It had felt lovely with him still inside her. As he moved off the bed and away from her, the feeling of abandonment was acute. And worrisome.

How could she ever live without this again? How could she ever live without *him*?

The prospect appalled her.

He'd gone to the bathroom. She could hear him in there, whistling. The shower taps were turned on and she was imagining him in there washing himself all over when suddenly he was standing in the doorway, stark naked and dripping wet.

'OK, get yourself in here, woman,' he said. 'Refresh time.'

Jessie wanted to. Desperately. But didn't that make her a desperate? She had to stay cool, and strong.

'You and I know what will happen if I get in the shower with you,' she pointed out with what she hoped was sufficient sophistication. 'And I couldn't possibly do it again. Not this soon. Besides, I'm getting hungry. I'll need something to eat soon.'

'Funny you should say that,' he quipped, a wicked gleam in his eyes.

Jessie's mouth opened, then closed again. He meant it. He actually meant it. Worse, the idea excited her. She was getting to be as wicked as he was.

'Do you want me to come over there and carry

you?' he challenged. 'I will if you don't get that delicious butt of yours off that bed in five seconds flat.'

The thought of his carrying her naked body in his arms was almost as thrilling as her going down on him in the shower.

She stayed right where she was, and six seconds later he swept her up into his masterful and muscular arms.

'Just before I forget to tell you,' he said as he carried her into the bathroom, 'I think you are the most beautiful, sexiest, loveliest woman I have ever met.'

His words startled her. But she tried not to let them turn her head—or her heart—too much. Men like Kane were always good with words.

'Knowing you, you're sure to be thinking I'm only interested in you for sex,' he went on. 'And I have to confess,' he added as he placed her down under the hot jets of water, 'that right at this moment, sex is pretty much my main focus.'

His hands reached up to smooth her hair back from her face whilst the water soaked it through.

Jessie had often seen movies where water was used as a symbol of eroticism. Now she knew why. There was something primal about standing naked with your lover under water. The way it ran down over your body, making you aware of every exposed curve and hidden orifice. It splashed inside her mouth, beat on her nipples, pooled in her navel and ran down between her buttocks, soaking her secret places before trickling down her inner thighs.

'But it's the same for you tonight, isn't it?' he

murmured as he cradled her face with his hands and looked deep into her dilated eyes. 'We need this, you and I. Need to do everything to each other. We have to get this out of the way first or we won't be able to think of anything else. I've dreamt about you like this all week. Naked and willing in my bed, and in my shower, and in every room of my house. I won't let you wear any clothes tonight, Jessie, not even when we're eating. You're going to stay naked for me. You're going to let me touch you whenever I want to, *take* you whenever I want to. Give me permission, beautiful Jessie. Tell me that you want that, too.'

'Yes,' she heard herself say from some darkly erotic far-off place. 'Yes…'

CHAPTER THIRTEEN

'WELL? How was it last night?' Dora asked when they finally caught up with each other over mid-morning coffee. 'I was too sleepy to ask you when you got home. Sorry. I hope you didn't think I was rude to leave like that.'

Jessie had actually been grateful. She'd staggered home around one, having declined Kane's offer to walk her to the door, using the excuse that it was late enough. But she must have looked a right mess with her hair all over the place and not a scrap of make-up remaining on her face. Anyone other than a half-asleep old lady would have known on sight that she'd been having sex all night.

Jessie swallowed at the memory. Not just sex. Hot sex. Incredible sex. Sex such as she'd never known before.

'I had a very enjoyable time,' she said with an amazingly straight face. 'The food at the restaurant was fabulous. You know that place down on the beach at Balmoral?'

Dora didn't, thankfully. She said she'd never been to Balmoral, either the suburb or the beach.

Jessie invented a menu from scraps of memory of the last time she was there, all the while trying not to think of the incredible meal she *had* had last night. The food hadn't been incredible. It was just a couple

144

of frozen dinners, washed down with white wine and finished off with a selection of melons. Incredible was the fact that they'd been naked whilst eating, and sharing one of the kitchen chairs, with her being forbidden to feed herself.

In hindsight, their various sexual encounters the previous night seemed decadent. But at the time, they'd simply been exciting.

'Where did you go afterwards?' Dora asked.

'Just back to his place for a while,' Jessie said nonchalantly.

'And?'

'He has a very nice house. Not unlike yours.'

'And?'

'It has a glorious view of the ocean and it's chock-full of antiques. Kane must be worth a fortune.'

'And?'

'And what?'

'Jessie Denton, did you or did you not go to bed with the man?'

Jessie blushed at this unexpectedly forthright question. 'Don't ask questions like that, Dora. Emily might hear.'

'Not at this distance, she won't,' Dora replied.

They were sitting at the small plastic table setting outside their communal laundry, which was a good way from where Emily was happily playing in her fig-tree cubby house.

Jessie sighed. 'Yes, I did,' she confessed.

'Good,' Dora pronounced. 'He's a really nice man.'

Jessie clenched her teeth hard in her jaw lest she

open her mouth and say something to disillusion Dora.

'And he really likes Emily,' Dora added.

'He divorced his wife because he didn't want children,' Jessie couldn't resist throwing into the conversation.

'What? Are you sure about that?'

'Positive. He told me so himself.'

'Strange. He doesn't act like a man who doesn't
like children. He's very patient, for starters. And
kind.'

'Maybe he just doesn't like babies. Emily is not a
baby.'

'True. But that's a shame. I thought he might have
been the one.'

'Which one is that?'

'The one who'll marry you and be a father to
Emily. She's very keen on that idea, you know.'

No, Jessie didn't know. 'You mean, on having a
father? She's never spoken about it to me. Emily
hasn't missed out on anything, not having a father,'
she argued defensively.

'How do you know? She's a deep little thinker,
your Emily. She sees other fathers coming to pick
up their children at the day-care centre. She might
have been wanting a father for ages, but didn't want
to say anything to upset you. She loves her mummy
a great deal but I think she'd love to have a daddy,
too. That's why Kane's been such a big hit with her.
And why she asked if you two were going to get
married last night.'

Jessie's heart turned over. It was already happening, what she'd feared all along. If she kept seeing Kane, Emily was going to get more and more attached to him and one day, poof, he'd be gone and her little girl would be broken-hearted. Her own broken heart she could cope with. She was a grown-up. But how could you explain to a four-year-old that adult relationships didn't always end in marriage? They usually just ended.

'He wants to take me and Emily out this Sunday,' Jessie said with a worried frown on her face. 'I'm going to have to call him and tell him no.' She should never have said yes in the first place. She was weak, weak, weak!

'But why, for pity's sake?'

'Because it's not fair on Emily, letting her think he really likes her. It's not Emily he wants, Dora. It's just me.'

'You don't know that. Ask him.'

'No. He'll only lie to me.'

Dora looked at her with shocked eyes. 'I knew you were cynical, Jessie. I didn't realise you were *that* cynical. For what it's worth, I think you're making a big mistake. He's a nice man and deserves a chance. Not only that, *you* deserve a chance. And Emily, too. Don't make hasty decisions. Give your relationship with Kane a bit of time. OK, so it might not work out, but if you don't try you'll never know. Life can be cruel but it can also be wonderful. You have to believe that or life isn't worth living. I was very lonely and depressed till you and Emily came along. In fact, I was in danger of being a miserable old witch of a woman, I was so full of regrets and resentments. But you brought some light into my life. You and Emily. You're a lovely girl, Jessie Denton, but where men are concerned you're way too hard. And way too distrustful. I've seen a lot of life and I'd put my money on Kane being a decent man. He might even change his mind about having children now that he's become involved with you and Emily. People can change, you know.'

Jessie didn't think that a man who divorced his wife over that single issue was likely to change. At the same time, she supposed she was being a bit hard on him. He'd really been wonderfully warm and considerate last night. He had the capacity to be a sensitive new-age guy as well; he was very capable in the kitchen. And he could give a massage like a professional. He made a great boyfriend and lover, even if not a husband and father.

She'd be out of her mind to voluntarily give him up. Just the thought of never experiencing again what she'd experienced last night made her feel sick. At the same time, she had to make some firm ground rules between them. No pretend family outings. No coming over till Emily was asleep at night. And no expecting her to stay at his place all night on the occasions they did go out.

There! That was reasonable.

Kane didn't think so when she rang him during Emily's after-lunch nap.

'You're being ridiculous again,' he growled. 'About everything. Jessie, I really like you. No, that's a lie. I love you, damn it.'

Jessie gasped into the phone.

'Yes, yes, I'm sure you don't believe me. But it's true.'

'It's you who's being ridiculous,' Jessie countered once she got over her shock. 'I know what you love, Kane Marshall, and it isn't the real me. It's the silly, weak woman I became last night. I don't know what got into me to let you do all those things. My only excuse is that I hadn't been with a man in such a long time. *And*, of course, you seemed to know just what to do to tap into my dark side.'

'Your *dark* side? I wasn't trying to tap into your dark side, sweetheart. Just your feminine side. That side you put on hold most of the time whilst you're being one tough mamma who thinks all men are lying scumbags who couldn't possibly love you or want you for anything other than sex. For pity's sake, I know you've been hurt by other men in the past. Your less than admirable father and that creep, Lyall. But that doesn't mean *all* men are bad. You don't like other people misjudging *you*, or jumping to conclusions over *your* morals, but you're only too ready to jump to conclusions over mine.'

Jessie winced. He was right. She knew he was right.

'You're a wonderful girl, Jessie,' he said more gently. 'But you really need to get that chip off your shoulder. I want you in my life. You *and* Emily. But you have to believe in me, and trust me. I don't know what else I can say to convince you that I'm sincere. Look, if you don't think you could ever love me back, then I suppose I'm just wasting my time. If last night was just you exorcising your sexual frustrations then I guess that's that, then. Just let me say that last night was the most incredible night of my life. You are everything I want in a woman and a lover, Jessie Denton.'

Jessie felt totally chastened by his speech. And moved. 'I…I thought last night was pretty incredible, too. I'm sorry I said what I said, Kane. And I'm sorry I'm such a bitch.'

He laughed. 'In a way, I like that about you. But I like the woman you were last night, too. They're both you, Jessie. And I love them both.'

'I wish you wouldn't keep saying that you love me.'

'Why?'

'Because I'm afraid of it.'

'Yes, I know that, sweetheart. But you're going to have to get used to it. I love you and I'm not going to go away.'

She was beginning to see that, his reassurance flooding through her heart like a giant wave, washing away some of those old fears, the ones where she did think no man would ever truly love and want her, not now that she had Emily. Her mother had drummed into her that no man really wanted another man's child.

But was he talking marriage here? She didn't like to ask. It was premature. And what about the matter of children? Dora could be right there. Maybe he would want children with her, if he loved her enough. If not, at least she already had Emily. And he seemed to genuinely like Emily.

'It might be nice if you told me what you feel for

me,' Kane inserted softly. 'I need some encouragement here.'

'I doubt you ever need encouragement when you want something, Kane Marshall.'

'I've never wanted something quite so unattainable before.'

'How can you say that after the way I acted last night? You said "jump" and I said "how high?"'

'That's just during sex. On a day-to-day basis, you're extremely difficult to handle. Now, am I allowed to come over today?'

'No.'

'How come I knew you were going to say that? What about tomorrow? Can I take you and Emily out, as I was going to?'

'Yes, but no sex.' This edict was more for her benefit than his. She was so tender down there, it wasn't funny.

'I wasn't expecting any. Besides, I'm knackered.'

'That's today. You'll be recovered by tomorrow.'

'You could be right. I'll be even more recovered by Monday.'

'Monday is a work day.'

'Yes, but there's always our lunch-hour. Karen always goes out and I have that lovely office—complete with that huge Chesterfield—all to myself.'

Jessie's cheeks burned at the thought. Just as well he couldn't see her. 'You don't honestly expect me to do that, do you?' she said, trying to sound shocked and not excited.

'A man can always hope.'

'Friday night is our date night,' she said primly. 'You'll have to wait till then.'

'Friday night is a definite, then? No excuses?'

'No excuses.'

'Next Friday night is the office Christmas party,' he told her in an amused tone. 'As the acting boss, I'm obliged to attend. As a new employee, I will expect you to be there too, in a sexy party dress.'

'You devil! You tricked me.'

'You should have remembered.'

'I'm not having you make love to me in your office.'

'You gave me your word. You told me you were a woman of your word.'

'That's emotional blackmail.'

'No one will notice if we slip away from time to time,' he said softly. 'My office is out of the way. And it has a lock on its door.'

'But I wouldn't be able to relax,' she protested. 'I'd be worried what people might be thinking.'

'Who cares what they think? After Christmas, I won't be the boss there any longer and no one will think a thing.'

'They'll always think you hired me because you fancied me.'

'Mmm. Could be true.'

'But it isn't! You know it isn't!'

'Yes, I know. I was only teasing. We'll be very discreet. Tell me you love me, Jessie Denton.'

'No.'

'But you know you do.'

'All I know is that you're a very arrogant man.

And far, far too sure of himself. You need pulling down a peg or two.'

'And you, missie, need a lot more loving.'

'Is that what they're calling it these days?'

'Would you rather I used a cruder term?'

'No.'

'Good, because I'm not just talking about sex. I'm talking loving in the wider context. You need everything a man who loves you can provide. You need caring for. And protection. And support. And security. You need someone there to help you when things go wrong, someone you can turn to and rely upon.'

Oh, how wonderful that would be, she thought with a deep sigh. But was it just a dream, a mad promise from a lust-crazed fool, or the offer of a man genuinely in love?

Jessie had been cynical too long to accept what Kane was offering without any wariness whatsoever.

'What you need,' Kane finished, 'is me.'

'Yes, I certainly do,' she agreed. 'You've revitalised my libido with a vengeance. But we'll both have to wait till Friday to tackle it.'

He swore. The first time he'd sworn in front of her.

'What you need, madam,' he ground out, 'is being put across my knee and having your bottom soundly smacked.'

'Ooh,' she said mockingly. 'Is that a promise or a threat?'

'You're full of bulldust, do you know that? You're scared stiff of me, that's the truth. You're scared stiff of what I can make you feel and what I can make you do. Come Friday night, you *will* tell me you love me. Right there, in that office. Even if I have to smack your bare bottom to get you to say it. And that's a promise!'

Jessie was speechless, her heart pounding at the images he evoked. And the feelings. This couldn't be love, she told herself. This was just lust. He'd totally corrupted her last night.

'That's not love,' she whispered shakily.

'What is it, then?'

'It's torture.'

'Aye, it's that too, till you surrender to it. I've surrendered to my feelings for you. So when are you going to do the same? No, don't answer that. I can be patient. Just remember I'm never going to let you go, Jessie Denton. You are mine. So get used to it.'

CHAPTER FOURTEEN

TEN o'clock Monday morning saw Kane sitting at Harry's desk, feeling quite satisfied with the way his relationship with Jessie was going. Yesterday, he'd proved to her that they didn't have to be making mad, passionate love to enjoy each other's company. He'd also showed her—at least he hoped he had—that he had the makings of a good father for Emily.

On the Saturday, he'd bought a child car seat so there'd be no objections to his driving them out to the rural outskirts of Sydney on the Sunday. After an hour's investigation on the internet, he'd found a horse-riding establishment that catered for children, and had other entertainment as well. Bouncy castles and the like.

Emily had enjoyed herself enormously, although by the time they arrived back home around six o'clock, she'd been very tired and a little out of sorts. She hadn't eaten much of the take-away pizzas Jessie had allowed him to buy this time, which Jessie said wasn't like her at all.

Kane had insisted on taking Emily's temperature— he'd heard horror stories of children coming down with meningitis lately—but her temperature proved to be normal. Jessie had said she was probably over-tired. They'd done a lot that day. After a bath, Kane had read Emily a story till she dropped off.

Afterwards, even though Jessie had let him stay, Kane had made no attempt to make love to her. He'd watched the Sunday-night movie with her—a Harrison Ford action thriller which could bear reviewing—and chatted about various topics during the ads. Books. Movies. Music. Kane had discovered she had a wide taste and knowledge of all three, which didn't really surprise him. She was a smart cookie. He'd known that from the first moment he looked into her eyes. She had intelligent eyes.

Although he'd been dying to make love to her, Kane had contented himself with a goodnight kiss. He suspected Jessie wouldn't have objected too much if he *had* seduced her, but he hadn't wanted to take the chance. She always seemed so quick to believe the worst of him.

By Friday, however, he wouldn't be capable of being so noble. He wouldn't be waiting till the party finished, either. Hell, no. Kane shuddered over the thought of how long this week would prove to be.

When the phone rang, he reached forward and snatched it up.

'Kane Marshall.'

'Kane, I have a problem.'

Kane snapped forward in his chair. It was Jessie, sounding worried.

'What is it? I thought you were here, at work.'

'I am. The day-care centre has just rung me. Emily has come down with conjunctivitis. Apparently, one of the other children had it on Friday. Anyway, because it's so contagious, they want me to go and pick her up.'

'That's fine, Jessie. You go. No problem. I'll square it with Michele.'

'That's just it. Michele's not here. She had an appointment with her obstetrician this morning, and she's relying on me to do this magazine layout by the time she gets back. I would really hate to let her down, Kane. I've tried to ring Dora but she's out, too. Lord knows where. She's usually home on a Monday. I *can* leave Emily at the centre but they'll put her in a room on her own. It's a kind of quarantine rule they have. They did this to her once before when I was working at the restaurant and she got very upset. She thought she was being punished. I...'

'I'll go get her, Jessie,' Kane immediately offered. 'Just ring them and let them know who I am and that you're giving me permission to pick Emily up. I'll take her to the doctor, too. Get her some drops for her eyes.'

'Would you, Kane? Would you really?'

Kane was amazed at the surprise in her voice. 'Yes, of course. It would be my pleasure. Poor Emily. There's nothing worse than having sore eyes. Does she have a regular doctor you take her to?'

'Not exactly. I always go to a nearby twenty-four-hour clinic. They bulk bill, but you have to be seen by whatever doctors are on call that day.'

Privately Kane resolved that little arrangement would change, once *he* was responsible for Jessie and Emily. And he aimed to be, one day. Still, that clinic would do for today.

'Right. I'll come and get her medicare card from you. Jot down the address of the clinic and I'll be on my way.'

Kane jumped to his feet and reached for his suit jacket straight away. It could only have been thirty seconds before he'd made it to Jessie's desk, where he was stunned to find her with tears running down her face.

'Jessie. Darling. What's up?' he said as he hunched down beside her chair. 'Why are you crying?'

She could not seem to speak, just buried her face in her hands.

'Jessie, talk to me. Tell me what's wrong.' He took her hands in his and lifted them to his lips.

She stared at him through soggy lashes. 'I've never known anyone like you,' she choked out. 'You can't be real.'

Relief zoomed through Kane, as well as the most ego-boosting pleasure. She wasn't unhappy. She was actually complimenting him with her tears.

But how sad that she would feel disbelief that a man would do something nice for her and her daughter.

'I'm real, all right,' he said with a soft smile. 'Just ask my mum. Now, stop being a silly billy, give me what I came for, then get back to work. You don't want everyone saying I hired a nincompoop just because I fancied her, do you?'

He liked it when a smile broke through her tears. God, but she was beautiful when she smiled. Her eyes glittered and her whole face came alive.

'We couldn't have that, could we?' she said, dashing the tears away with her fingers.

'Absolutely not.'

'OK. Here's the medicare card and the clinic's address. Now, what are you going to do with Emily after you've been to the doctor? They didn't say she was actually sick, but perhaps she should go home. I could give you the keys to the granny flat if you wouldn't mind staying with her. There's plenty of food in the fridge and the cupboards. She usually has a sleep after lunch. If she gets bored or stroppy, she likes to watch videos. She has a whole pile of them in the cabinet under the TV.'

'Sounds good to me. I'll give you a call when I get there, and I'll wait with her till you come home.'

'I don't know what to say, Kane,' she said as she drew her keys out of her handbag. 'Are you sure you can manage? I mean…you haven't much experience looking after kids on your own.'

'I happen to be an extremely devoted uncle, so you're wrong there. What do you think I did on Saturday night when you wouldn't let me come over? I minded the two terrors so that their parents could go out and relax together. Actually, I don't know what their mother complains about. They were as good as gold. Of course, I plied them with junk food and lollies till they fell asleep on the sofa in front of the TV. Then I carried them up to bed. Works every time,' he said with a quick grin.

'Now, don't you worry,' he added. 'I'm more than capable of looking after Emily. And I won't feed her junk food, or lollies. To be honest, it'll be a pleasant change from sitting at that damned desk, pretending to work. Things wind down leading up to Christmas. My entire workload this week is choosing what grog to buy for the Christmas party. *Very* challenging.'

He stood up, pocketing her keys and picking up the medicare card and piece of paper with the address. 'I'll call, OK? And don't worry.'

'I won't,' she said, looking much more composed. 'I can't tell you how grateful I am.'

Kane threw her one last smile and whirled on his heels.

Nothing made a man feel better, he decided as he strode manfully away, than being able to help the woman he loved.

Jessie worked hard and fast for the next few hours, not leaving her desk till the magazine layout looked perfect. To her, anyway.

Michele returned shortly after she'd finished, and only minutes after Kane had rung saying he was at the flat with Emily and that her conjunctivitis wasn't too bad. He'd already put one lot of drops in, they'd shared Vegemite toast and a glass of milk, followed by a banana each. Now they were settling down to watch *The Lion King*.

With her worries about her daughter waylaid, Jessie could focus on Michele's reaction to her work. When Michele started frowning, Jessie's alarm grew. Maybe the layout wasn't as good as she thought it was.

'I would never have imagined doing it this way at all,' Michele said at last, tipping her head from side to side as she studied the computer screen. 'But yes, I like it! You are very creative, Jessie. Kane's found a real gem in you. Harry's going to be delighted at your joining his staff.'

Jessie sighed her relief. 'Thank you. But…would you mind if I left now?' she asked hurriedly. 'I know it's only two o'clock, but my little girl has conjunctivitis. The day-care centre rang and wanted me to go get her straight away, but I didn't feel I could without finishing the layout first.'

'That was very professional of you, Jessie. But honestly, I would have understood. That kind of thing happens to me all the time. And yes, of course you can go. I hope your little girl is OK.'

Jessie didn't want to tell her about Kane coming to the rescue. That was her own personal business.

'I'm sure she will be,' Jessie said, standing up hurriedly and getting her things together. 'Thanks, Michele. I did work through my lunch-hour. And I'm happy to do some extra work at home to make up for the extra hour and a half.'

'Are you kidding me? You've achieved more here in less than a day than your predecessor would have done in a week!'

Jessie laughed and left.

The day outside wasn't overly hot, but it was humid, Jessie's blouse sticking to her back as she hurried to the train station. Sydney in December could be very sticky.

The train she caught was quite crowded, Jessie

lucky to get a seat. But she was still pressed up against other people, and the air-conditioning didn't seem to be working too well. Everywhere seemed crowded at the moment, even outside of peak hours. Lots of people doing Christmas shopping, she supposed.

Jessie was glad she'd finished hers. She had Emily's Felicity Fairy doll and accessories all wrapped up and hidden on a high shelf in one of Dora's wardrobes, along with a few little cheaper gifts she'd bought during the year. She'd long sent her mother's card and gift to Ireland. A lovely set of linen serviettes and holders that her mother would probably put away and never use. Truly, she was a difficult woman to buy anything for.

For Dora, she'd bought some place mats and matching coasters in a blue and white willow pattern. She hadn't spent as much money on her as her mother, but she knew Dora would appreciate the gift more, and actually use it. Dora loved that willow pattern. She had a tea set in it, a vase and a large serving plate.

It came to Jessie during the train ride home that she hadn't bought Kane anything. In truth, his rather sudden intrusion into her life had driven Christmas from her mind, which was ironic given what she'd said to Dora that night before she'd gone to the bar. Hadn't she wanted a man for Christmas, some gorgeous guy who'd give her a good time?

Kane had certainly done just that, and more. Much more.

Jessie still found it incredible that he loved her.

But he said he did and she had no real reason to doubt him. Frankly, she didn't *want* to doubt him any more. She was tired of her cynicism, tired of trying to stop herself from falling in love with him. Dora was right. Life could be cruel but it could be wonderful.

Kane was a wonderful man, despite his not wanting children of his own. Why he didn't she had no idea, but she would certainly ask him. Soon.

And if he still insists he doesn't, Jessie, where can this relationship go? You would want children with the man you loved. And you do love him, don't you? That was one of the reasons you were crying earlier. Because you knew you couldn't stop yourself loving him any longer.

You love him and you'd make any compromise just to be with him.

But maybe you're jumping the gun here, Jessie Denton.

Maybe he just wants to continue being your boyfriend and your lover. Maybe he doesn't want to live with you, or marry you. Maybe the way it is now is all he'll ever want.

Dismay clutched at Jessie's heart. It wasn't enough. Just seeing him on a Friday night. And occasionally at the weekend. Not enough at all.

But it would have to be enough. She couldn't force him to want marriage, let alone children. She couldn't force him to do anything.

Unless…

No, no, that wasn't right. She would not try to trap him with a baby. It wouldn't work, anyway. The man

who'd written *Winning at Work* would never suc-
cumb to that kind of emotional blackmail. He was
strong on his beliefs, be they right or wrong.

The train pulling into Roseville brought a swift
end to her mental toing and froing. During her hurried walk home Jessie told herself she should stop
questioning everything and just live one day at a time
for a while. Things were good in her life at the moment. Kane was good for her. And he was good for
Emily. Why risk what they had by wanting more?
She was a fool.

'Sssh,' Kane said when she burst in through the
back door. 'Emily's asleep. She nodded off during
the video and I carried her into bed. But that was
only ten minutes ago. Gosh, you look hot.'

'I am hot. It's terribly sticky outside.' The granny
flat was nicely cool, with double insulation in the
roof and fans in the high ceilings. Kane looked very
cool, sitting on the sofa with his arms running along
the back of the sofa and his long legs stretched out
before him, crossed at the ankles. Very cool and very
sexy.

Suddenly, Jessie felt even hotter.

'I'll have to have a shower and change,' she said
hurriedly. 'Once Emily's asleep, usually nothing
wakes her up, so we don't have to creep about. I
won't be long,' she said, and fled into the bedroom.

Emily stayed blessedly asleep whilst her mother
stripped off, showered then pulled on a simple cotton
sundress in pink and white checks, which looked sexier on her than she realised.

*   *   *

Kane gritted his teeth when she emerged, thinking to himself that he'd better make himself scarce, or all his resolutions about not touching her till Friday were about to fly out the window. But when he rose and reached for his jacket, which was draped over a kitchen chair, her face betrayed that his leaving was the last thing she wanted.

They stared at each other for a long moment. And then she said something that floored him. His mouth literally dropped open.

'Say that again,' he blurted out, not daring to believe what he thought he'd heard.

'I love you,' she repeated, her face flushed, her eyes glistening.

Kane knew that in years to come, he would always remember that moment. A dozen different emotions warred for supremacy. Disbelief? Shock? Joy? Delight? Satisfaction? Desire?

Desire won in the end. Or was it just his own love for her? How could you not take a woman into your arms who'd just told you she loved you with such moving simplicity?

She went without any hesitation this time, not a trace of doubt in her face any more.

But he didn't kiss her straight away. He looked down into those beautiful eyes and savoured the sincerity he saw in their depths.

'When did you decide this?' he said softly.

'On the way home on the train.'

'A very good place to make decisions.'

'Much better than when I'm like this,' she told him

with a small smile. 'I can't think straight when I'm in your arms.'

'That's good to know as well.'

Her arms slid even tighter around his neck, pulling their bodies hard against each other. 'Aren't you going to kiss me?' she asked breathlessly.

'Soon.'

'You have a sadistic side to you, Kane Marshall.'

'I never claimed to be a saint.'

Neither was he a masochist. His mouth was within a millimetre of contacting hers when there was a knock on the door.

His head lifted, and they groaned together.

It was Dora, all a-flutter.

'I saw Kane's car out the front,' she said. 'Is anything wrong?'

Jessie gave her a quick run-down on the little drama with Emily. Dora looked relieved.

'I'm so glad it's nothing serious. And that Kane could help. Sorry I wasn't here, dear. But you'll never guess what's happened.'

Kane and Jessie exchanged a look that carried both amusement and exasperation.

'Why don't I make us all some coffee,' Jessie said, 'and you can tell us what's happened?'

Kane suppressed a sigh and pulled out a kitchen chair for Dora, sitting down himself once the old lady was settled.

Apparently she'd received an unexpected call from her brother that morning, the one who hadn't been much support to her during their mother's last years. Dora hadn't spoken to him for a good two years.

'If it hadn't been Christmas I wouldn't have spoken to him today, either,' she said defiantly. 'But I'm so glad I did.'

Apparently, her brother explained how he'd been inundated with business and family problems when their mum had been ill, but admitted that he knew he hadn't done enough. He'd recently had a health scare himself and had been thinking that he wanted to make it up to Dora. The upshot was he'd come and taken Dora out to lunch, over which he'd asked her to go to his place for Christmas, and for the week afterwards, right up to New Year. It seemed his business was doing very well now; he owned a couple of cafés down around the Wollongong area on the south coast. He had a huge holiday house down there, and every one of their relatives was coming.

Kane saw Jessie's face fall at this news, and guessed that she and Emily always spent Christmas with Dora. After all, she had no one else. It was just the opportunity he'd been waiting for.

'That's great, Dora,' he piped up. 'And it sure takes a load off Jessie's mind. You see, I asked her and Emily to come spend Christmas with me and my family. But she was worried sick about you, thinking you'd be all alone. Of course, you'd have been welcome to come too, but this solves everything much better.'

Dora seemed relieved and pleased at this announcement, whilst Jessie went a little quiet. After Dora bustled off to go do some more Christmas shopping, Kane was left to face a slightly cool Jessie.

'What a smooth liar you are,' she said.

Kane could feel the doubts rising in her again.

'There's nothing wrong with little white lies, Jessie,' he pointed out. 'Especially when they're partially true. I was going to ask you to spend Christmas with me.'

'*And* with your family?'

'Yes.'

'And what were you going to introduce me as?'

'What would you like me to introduce you as?'

'I don't know. You tell me.'

'How about fiancée?'

She stared at him and he sighed. 'I guess that is rushing you somewhat. How about my new girlfriend, then?'

Jessie just kept shaking her head, her expression bewildered. 'Were you seriously asking me to marry you? You weren't joking?'

'I wouldn't joke about something like that.'

'But we've only known each other ten days!'

'I know I love you and I know you love me.'

'But we don't really *know* each other.'

'I beg to differ. I know you very well. Much better than I knew Natalie when I married her, and we'd been dating for months. The problem is you don't think you know me. But you had the wrong picture of me from the start. I rather hoped I'd managed to get rid of that poor image by now, but it seems I haven't.'

'That's not true. I...I think you're wonderful. You must know that. But *marriage*? That's a very big step, Kane. For one thing, we don't agree on one very important issue. The same issue you didn't agree on with your first wife.'

'*What?* You mean *you* don't want children, either? Hell, Jessie, I thought…' A great black pit yawned open in Kane's stomach. He could not believe it. Jessie didn't want his children. The woman he loved. The woman he adored. How cruel was that?

Jessie blinked. Had she heard that right? His *ex* hadn't wanted children? But that couldn't be right. She'd said she was pregnant that day in Kane's office and that she was keeping the baby. Of course, lots of women who didn't think they wanted children changed their minds once they actually got pregnant. But if that was the case…

'Hold it there,' she said. 'Why, exactly, did you divorce Natalie?'

'Mainly because she refused to have children. But I think I also realised I didn't really love her.'

'Oh!' Jessie exclaimed with a gasp. 'I thought it was *you* who didn't want children!'

'*Me?* I love children. How on earth did you get that ridiculous idea? I thought I explained the reasons behind my divorce quite clearly.'

'You told me you disagreed with your wife over the matter of having children and I just assumed it had to be you who didn't want kids.' Jessie felt truly chastened. But secretly elated. 'I'm so sorry, Kane. My old prejudice against men again.'

He nodded, unable to feel unhappy, now that he knew Jessie wanted more children. 'An understandable mistake.'

'So you really do want children?'

'A whole tribe of them, if possible. The more the merrier.'

Jessie beamed. 'Me, too.'

'What about your career?'

'My career would never come before my kids. But hopefully I could juggle both.'

Kane's delight was as great as his despair had been. 'In that case, come here, woman, and make it up to me for thinking such dreadful things.'

She ran into his arms. This time, he actually got to kiss her for five seconds before they were interrupted.

'Mummy...'

They pulled apart to find Emily standing in the bedroom doorway, rubbing her eyes.

'Hello, sweetie,' her mother said. 'You feeling better now?'

'I'm thirsty. And my eyes are sore.'

Jessie gave a small sigh. 'I'll get you a drink of water. Kane, where are those eye drops?'

'Over here on the coffee-table. I'll get them.'

Their eyes clashed momentarily, Kane seeing that Jessie was watching him for signs of impatience.

Instead, he smiled, then hurried over to sweep Emily up into his arms. 'Did you have a good sleep, princess?'

She tipped her head on one side. 'Were you kissing Mummy just then?'

Jessie stopped breathing.

'I sure was,' Kane said. 'It was very nice, too. Do you mind my kissing Mummy?'

'No. Will you kiss me, too?'

He laughed and planted a peck on her forehead.
'There. Now let me get those eye drops into you.'

'Do you *have* to?' she wailed.

'Yes. I *have* to,' Kane returned firmly.

Jessie heaved a great sigh of happiness. Even
more wonderful than everything which had happened
today was having someone else put Emily's eye
drops in.

CHAPTER FIFTEEN

WORK the following Friday came to a halt by lunch-time, at which point the males on the staff pitched in to transform the main office floor into party land. Several of the central cubicles were dismantled to provide a more than adequate dance floor. Desks were cleared and decorations and disco lights went up.

Peter—who apparently loved playing DJ each year—set about filling his area with his latest hi-fi gear, whistling *Jingle Bells* as he worked. Kane and Karen took charge of stocking up the temporary bar, whilst Margaret roped Jessie and Michele into help-ing her with the food, which they spread out, buffet-style, on several desks pushed together. A local ca-tering company had supplied a wide selection of cold meats, seafood and salads, with some delicious cream-topped cakes for the sweet tooths, plus loads of snacks.

Jessie thought that there was way too much to eat and drink for their small staff, but when she re-marked on this to Michele, she was informed that their office party was so popular that loads of other people in the building came, along with clients, past and present.

'And everyone's other halves usually drop in as well,' Michele added. 'Tyler's sure to be late, work-

172

aholic that he is, but he'll make an appearance at some stage, even if only to see me safely home.'

Tyler, Jessie knew by now, was Michele's husband.

'And speaking of other halves,' Michele said after a glance over at Kane, 'yours is looking very bright-eyed and bushy-tailed tonight. What *have* you been doing to him, girl?'

Absolutely nothing of what Michele was implying. There'd been no actual lovemaking, despite their spending every evening this week together. Kane didn't seem to mind stopping at a goodnight kiss. He'd even promised he wouldn't press her for more in any shape or form here at the party tonight.

'He does look yummy in black, doesn't he?' Jessie said with that swirl in her stomach that always occurred whenever she looked at the man she loved. It had been difficult controlling her own desires these past few days, but it had been more important to her to know that Kane's love was not just sexually based than to indulge in some passing pleasure.

'You haven't told anyone else here about our being engaged, have you?' she added swiftly. She didn't mind Michele knowing. They were fast becoming firm friends and she just couldn't keep her good news totally secret.

Still, it was good that Kane hadn't bought her a ring yet. That way he couldn't be annoyed with her for not wearing it at work. Jessie was still worried over what the other people at Wild Ideas might think.

'No. I haven't told anyone else,' Michele said with a sigh. 'But if you keep looking at each other the way you do, people will begin to suspect something is going on.'

Kane turned his head at that moment, and their eyes connected. His smile carried so much obvious love that Jessie could see what Michele meant.

'OK, everyone!' Kane announced to the room. 'Everything's ready for the party. Time for the girls to go and put their glad rags on. The guys too, if you've brought something more colourful to change into.' He glanced at his watch. 'At three o'clock, the doors will be thrown open and it'll be all systems go. Though speaking of systems, please make sure that your computers are safely turned off, passwords hidden and all important files discreetly locked away. I don't want Harry coming home and finding that all your wonderfully wild ideas have been stolen, or sabotaged. OK?'

'OK, boss!' they all chorused, Jessie included.

How proud of him she felt, this wonderful, gorgeous, sensible-thinking man who loved her.

Twenty minutes later, she was nervously viewing herself in the full-length mirror that hung on the back of the ladies' room door. Her cocktail dress was brand new, and very sexy. Black silk with turquoise swirls on it, it had a halter neckline, a wide, extremely tight waistband and a swishy skirt.

Her shoes were new, too. Turquoise, in the currently fashionable slip-on style, which showed off her pretty ankles and scarlet-painted toenails. This time she'd been able to afford fake tan, so her bare legs and arms glowed a nice honey colour. Her hair was down for once, and not too bushy, courtesy of the more expensive hair products she could also now buy and which tamed the frizz somewhat. She was wearing more make-up than she would usually wear in the office as well, and considerably less under-wear. No bra for starters and just the briefest thong underneath.

'Wow!' Margaret said when she saw her.

'Yes, wow!' Karen agreed.

Michele just raised her eyebrows in a knowing fashion.

Kane's reaction when he saw her was not quite as enthusiastic. He wasn't too pleased, either, when Jessie was subjected to instant male attention. The men flocked around her, getting her drinks, constantly asking her to dance and pretending to be devastated when she refused.

Jessie suspected Kane was jealous, but if so, why did he keep his distance? Why didn't *he* come and ask her to dance? She wouldn't have said no to him.

Finally, after the party had been raging for over two hours, he walked over to her, his expression tight.

'Could I have a private word, Jessie?'

'Of course,' she replied, and threw her circle of admirers a bright smile. 'Won't be long.'

Kane's grip on her elbow was firm as he steered her away from the party and along the corridor towards his office. Jessie quivered inside at his force-fulness, but it was a quiver of excitement, not nerves. A few glasses of champagne had dispensed with her earlier worries, replacing them with a deliciously carefree attitude.

'I said I wasn't going to do this, remember?' she remarked blithely, all the while quite happy with the prospect of being ravished on Kane's desk.

'I haven't brought you here for sex,' Kane snapped as he banged the door shut behind them.

'Oh…'

'Look, I know you're worried about the rest of the staff thinking you weren't hired on your merits. And I've tried damned hard tonight not to embarrass you by staking my claim on you publicly. But you *are* my woman, Jessie,' he pronounced firmly. '*Mine*. And it's time everyone out there knew that.'

'Oh…'

'I've asked you to marry me and you've said yes. You should be wearing my ring.'

'But…'

'No buts. I'm tired of your buts.' With that he drew a blue velvet box out of his jacket pocket and flipped it open. 'I hope you like it.'

Jessie stared down at the solitaire diamond engagement ring, then swallowed. Oh, God, she was going to cry. 'It…it's beautiful,' she stammered.

'*You're* beautiful,' he said thickly, and taking the ring out of the box, he put the box back in his pocket, then came forward and picked up her left hand.

'I love you, Jessie Denton,' he said as he slipped it on her trembling ring finger.

Her eyes flooded, then tears spilled over, running down her cheeks. 'And I love you,' she choked out.

He wiped the tears away with his spare hand, then bent to kiss each wet cheek. 'That's nothing to cry about,' he said with a soft smile in his voice. 'At least, I hope not.'

'Oh, no,' she denied hotly. 'Never!'

With a rush of sweet emotion, Jessie wound her arms up around his neck and pulled him close. 'You mean the world to me!' she proclaimed.

His hesitation was only slight before he kissed her. Soon, there was no hesitation, only passion. His kisses were fierce, his clasp so tight around her back that her breasts were totally flattened against his chest.

His sudden wrenching away came as a shock.

'Sorry,' he ground out. 'I promised I wouldn't do that.'

She loved it that he cared enough about her to stop. But the time for testing him further was long over.

'It's all right, Kane. I *want* you to make love to me.'

'What? You mean…*here*?'

'Yes, here. Now.'

He watched, gaze smouldering as she kicked off her shoes then reached up under her skirt to peel her panties off. That done, she untied the bow at the back of her neck, letting the straps fall so that her bare breasts were exposed.

When Kane sucked in sharply, her stomach quivered and her already erect nipples tightened further.

'I'd better lock the door,' he rasped.

He did so, then took her hand and led her over to the nearby Chesterfield. There, he drew her down onto his lap, kissing her and playing with her breasts till she was breathless and shaking. Only then did he slide one hand up under her skirt.

'No,' she protested. 'No, I don't want that, Kane. I want you. With nothing between us.'

'But…'

'No buts. It's all right. It's a safe time in my cycle. And if I'm wrong, what does it matter? I love you. You love me. We're getting married. A baby would be just fine.'

Kane could not believe the impact of her words. She must really love him and trust him, if she didn't mind conceiving his baby before they were married. He could not ask for more.

How he wanted her! His lovely Jessie. His woman.

He groaned at the first contact of their naked bodies, then moaned when his flesh began to enter hers. The look on her face as she sank all the way downwards told him she felt very much what he was feeling. When her hands cradled his face and she looked deep into his eyes, it took all of his will-power not to weep.

'I love you,' she whispered, and began to rise and fall upon him in a voluptuously sensual rhythm. 'I love you,' she repeated, pressing tiny kisses all over his face at the same time.

Kane closed his eyes in defence of the emotion that ripped through him. Never in his life had he felt anything like what this woman could make him feel. He could not wait to marry her, to promise to love and cherish her till death did them part. Because nothing short of death would destroy their union.

They were as one, not just in their bodies but also in their minds. She was going to be his soul mate. His best friend. The mother of his children.

When he took her hands from around his face and held them to his lips, she stopped moving to stare at him with glazed eyes.

'I...I never thought it could be like this,' she said in a voice that betrayed some lingering bewilderment over their relationship.

'I don't think it is very often,' he returned. 'We're very lucky.'

'Yes,' she agreed. 'Very.'

'We're going to go back to the party afterwards and announce our engagement,' he commanded, taking full advantage of the moment.

Jessie nodded. 'Yes. All right. But Kane...about tomorrow night...'

Kane frowned. 'What about tomorrow night?' She and Emily were supposed to be coming to sleep over at his house. It was Christmas Eve. He'd already bought a Christmas tree. A real one. And loads of decorations, which he planned on putting up with Emily. Not to mention more presents than was wise.

But how often did a man fall in love and get an instant family, one that probably hadn't been spoiled as he intended to spoil them, if he was allowed to?

'Don't tell me you've changed your mind about coming!'

She laughed a wicked little laugh. 'I'll be coming all right. Tonight. But Kane...about tomorrow night. I know it's probably old-fashioned of me, but I won't sleep in your bed with Emily in the same house. Not until we're married.'

Kane wasn't going to argue with her. Not at this precise moment. 'Fine,' he said. 'But I give you the right to change your mind again.'

'I won't change my mind this time.'

'We'll see,' he said, taking hold of her hips and urging her to start moving again.

When she cried out in naked ecstasy, Kane suspected he was in there with a pretty good chance.

CHAPTER SIXTEEN

'LOOK, Mummy, it's a Felicity Fairy doll!' Emily squealed as she ripped off the rest of the wrapping paper. 'And her horse! And her castle!'

'What a lucky girl you are,' Jessie replied from where she was curled up in the corner of Kane's sofa, dressed in the red silk nightie and robe Kane had given her on the stroke of midnight last night. They'd been up late talking and wrapping presents for Emily.

Of course, he'd insisted on seeing Jessie in his gift, one thing had led to another and, well…at least she hadn't actually slept in his bed. This room, however, had been witness to some torrid but tender lovemaking between even more provocative present-giving: perfume, body lotion and chocolates, which he'd fed her one by one as rewards for various services rendered.

Around one o'clock, a sated Jessie had given Kane the gifts she'd bought him. A book about the teachings of the Dalai Lama, a Robbie Williams CD and a DVD of the *Lord of the Rings* trilogy. She'd gleaned his taste from their many talks. He'd been so overcome that he had to listen to the CD and watch some of the DVD before making love to her again as a thank-you.

Shortly before three, a totally spent Jessie had stumbled into the second guest room, climbed into the bed and fallen into a deep sleep, where she had remained, not moving an inch, till Emily started tugging on her hair around six, saying Santa had been and Mummy just had to get up.

After Jessie had opened a single bleary eye, Emily had rushed off, saying she would wake Kane up, too.

That had been about fifteen minutes ago.

Jessie yawned just as Kane came into the living room with two mugs of freshly brewed coffee. He was actually wearing clothes. Shorts and a T-shirt. He needed a shave but he looked good like that. Very sexy.

'I really need this,' she said as she took one of the mugs and cradled it in her hands. 'It's just as well you took me to meet your family the other night when I looked all right. I look like something the cat dragged in today.'

'You look beautiful,' he said, and bent to give her a peck on the forehead before settling next to her. 'Glowing, in fact. Being in love suits you.'

Jessie glanced down at her engagement ring then up at the man who'd given it to her. 'Being in love with *you* suits me,' she said. 'You are the most incredible man.'

'But of course!' He grinned. 'Didn't I tell you that from the start?'

She laughed. 'You're also very arrogant.'

'Not true. I just know what I want when I see it.'

'Mummy, look at this!' Emily said, holding up the prettiest pink dress. 'Isn't it beautiful? I'm going to wear it when we visit Kane's mummy and daddy. I'll look like a princess, won't I, Kane?'

'Indeed.'

Jessie's heart turned over at how happy her daughter was. Kane had brought joy to both their lives, as well as the promise of a secure future.

'So, did Santa bring you everything you asked him for?' Jessie asked her daughter.

'Oh, yes,' Emily said, surveying all her new toys and clothes and games. 'He didn't forget a thing.'

'What do you like most?' Jessie asked, knowing exactly what her daughter would say: the Felicity Fairy doll.

'I like my new daddy the most,' came her unexpected reply. 'Can I call you Daddy now, Kane?' she added, crinkling her forehead up into a frown.

'I'd like nothing better, princess. Now, come over here,' he said as he put his coffee down on a sidetable, 'and give your new daddy a hug.'

Emily smiled as only a child could smile, then ran into Kane's waiting arms.

Jessie frowned.

'Emily,' she said once her daughter was comfortable on Kane's lap, her arms tightly wound around his neck, 'did you ask Santa for a new daddy that day at the shops?'

'Yes,' came the reply. 'You said if I was a good girl he would get me anything I asked for. And he did.'

Jessie blinked at Kane, who shrugged. 'The ways of the lord are very mysterious.'

She stared at him. 'I didn't know you were religious.'

'I'm not overly. But I think we might pop into a church later today, just to say thank you.'

'Can I go to church with you, Daddy?'

'But of course, princess. That's what daddies are for. To do whatever our little girls want us to do. And our big girls, too,' he added with a sexy wink Jessie's way.

'Next year,' Emily said excitedly, 'I'm going to ask Santa for a baby brother.'

'What a good idea,' Kane replied whilst Jessie tried not to choke on her coffee. 'I'm sure Santa won't have any trouble with that order. Though you have to remember that even Santa can't order the sex of a baby. That's up to God.'

'Then I'll ask God.'

'Go straight to the top. Excellent thinking. What do you think, Mummy?'

'I think we should clear away all that paper over there, then have a shower and get dressed.'

Emily pulled a face when her mother got up and went over to start picking up the mounds of Christmas paper.

'Mummies aren't as much fun as daddies,' she pronounced.

Kane smiled. 'Oh, I don't know, Emily. Your mummy has her moments. And she is a very good mummy, isn't she?'

'Oh, yes,' Emily said, and smiled over at her mother.

Jessie thought her heart would burst with happiness. She didn't know what she had done to deserve such happiness but she resolved never to take it for granted, to work hard, to always be a good wife to Kane, and an even better mother to Emily and whatever other children she might be blessed with.

Her mother was going to be surprised when she rang her later today and told her that some man did want to marry her, even with some other man's baby.

But of course Kane wasn't some man. He was a very special man.

'Daddy,' Emily whispered to Kane, 'why is Mummy crying?'

'She's crying because she's happy, princess,' he told Emily, a lump in his own throat. 'Grown-ups cry sometimes when they're happy.'

'When I cry, Mummy kisses me better.'

Kane nodded. 'What a good idea. Let's go kiss her better.'

EPILOGUE

ROBERT WILLIAM MARSHALL arrived just after midnight on Christmas Eve the following year, much to the delight of his big sister, Emily, who immediately started planning her next year's wish list, which included a pony, a boyfriend for Dora and a visit from her Nanna in Ireland, who'd been writing to her a lot since she'd become something called a Buddhist.

Within a few hours of her beautiful boy's arrival, Jessie decided work could go hang for a while. As much as she had enjoyed her time at Wild Ideas—and she'd worked till she was eight months pregnant—she felt the time had come for an extended maternity leave.

No doubt she would go back to work at some stage. Maybe she'd even start up her own boutique advertising company, run from home. When she mentioned this to Kane he was all for it, as long as he could become her partner.

When a fluttery and flushed Dora visited later that day with her new lodger on her arm—an aspiring writer in his sixties who'd never been married—Jessie and Kane exchanged knowing looks whilst Emily wondered if Santa and God had read her mind and simply got in early.

Jessie was allowed to bring the baby home on Boxing Day, which they spent at her in-laws' place.

She felt remarkably well, but it was still lovely to be waited on, and fussed over. Kane's mother could not stop picking up the baby and goo-gooing over him.

'Happy, darling?' Kane asked her when they finally went home that night and both their babies were asleep.

'Couldn't be happier,' Jessie replied.

'Care for a dance with your husband?' he said, and put on a suitable CD.

As Jessie went into her husband's arms, she remembered the first night they'd met, and danced.

Was it destiny that had brought them together?

It would be romantic to think so.

But it wouldn't be destiny that kept them together.

It would be love.

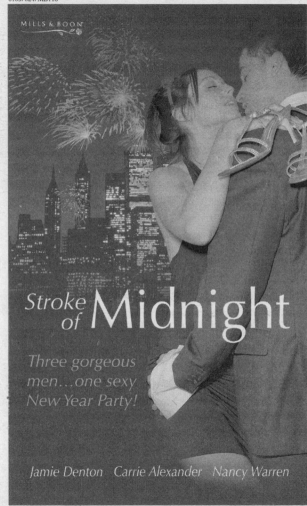

MILLS & BOON®

Volume 7
on sale from
2nd January
2005

Lynne
Graham

International Playboys

Crime of

Passion

4 Books
and a surprise gift!

We would like to take this opportunity to thank you for reading this Mills &
Boon® book by offering you the chance to take FOUR more specially
selected titles from the Modern Romance™ series absolutely FREE! We're also
making this offer to introduce you to the benefits of the Reader Service™—

* ★ **FREE home delivery**
* ★ **FREE gifts and competitions**
* ★ **FREE monthly Newsletter**
* ★ **Exclusive Reader Service offers**
* ★ **Books available before they're in the shops**

Accepting these FREE books and gift places you under no obligation to buy,
you may cancel at any time, even after receiving your free shipment. Simply
complete your details below and return the entire page to the address below.
You don't even need a stamp!

YES! Please send me 4 free Modern Romance books and a surprise gift. I
understand that unless you hear from me, I will receive 6 superb new
titles every month for just £2.69 each, postage and packing free. I am under
no obligation to purchase any books and may cancel my subscription at any
time. The free books and gift will be mine to keep in any case.

P4ZEF

Ms/Mrs/Miss/Mr ....Initials....................................

BLOCK CAPITALS PLEASE

Surname ....

Address...

....

....................................Postcode..

Send this whole page to:
UK: FREEPOST CN81, Croydon, CR9 3WZ